ON THE RUN

Laura ran a finger around the sweaty waistband of her slacks, just to reassure herself that the pouch containing the flash drive was still there. She'd left one with the article on it on Adam's desk yesterday, but this one also contained the names of her contacts and sources. All Adam had to do was run the article.

Run the article, Adam, she prayed. *Run it, and I'll be safe.*

Once the article ran—under her byline—there would be no point to her death. In fact, her death would turn the law's thoughtful eye on Johnny Tucker.

Oh no, once that article ran, Johnny T. would want her hale and hearty. But if he could prevent the article from appearing... and if she were to disappear...

She reached for her cup and spilled half of it before she managed to control her trembling.

NOVELS BY THE AUTHOR

ON HER TRAIL

by

MARCELLE DUBÉ

FALCON
RIDGE
PUBLISHING

ON HER TRAIL

Falcon Ridge Publishing
On Her Trail copyright © 2010 by Marcelle Dubé
Originally published in 2010 by Carina Press
Cover image copyright © littleny via Depositphotos
Cover copyright © 2018 Marcelle Dubé
and Falcon Ridge Publishing

Second edition
ISBN: 978-1-987937-21-3

Falcon Ridge Publishing
www.falconridgepublishing.com
marcelle.dube@gmail.com

ON HER TRAIL

by

MARCELLE DUBÉ

CHAPTER ONE

Fay Thorsen sat on the log bench at the top of the cliff and tried not to think about ghosts.

The sky was September blue, the hardened blue that came with cold mornings and warm afternoons. Wisps of clouds traveled high and fast, heading south. Soon the swans would follow, beating their powerful wings, gliding just below the top of the cliff. Their haunting cries would fade like dreams in the night as they followed the river to warmth.

Closing her eyes, Fay tilted her face upward. The sun was still warm, though every day it grew colder and more distant.

The Yukon River thundered below, but she was too far from the edge of the cliff to see the water. She opened her eyes and turned her head slightly, and there was the river in the distance, a shimmering ribbon of glory twisting between palisades of earth and rock.

Without moving her head, she shifted her gaze to the trees at the top of the cliff. Yes, there he was. Sawyer Leduc, standing in her woods, looking as young as the last time she had seen him thirty-four years ago, before he disappeared.

And at the other end of Fay's bench, as insubstantial as the ghost in the trees, sat James—husband, friend and punishment—dead now for three long months, but looking as he had all those years ago, when they were all young, and life was so complicated.

Fay breathed deeply of the scent of sweet clover carried on the wind.

She might as well appreciate the last of the fall before she lost her mind entirely.

* * *

Laura stepped out of the condo elevator, pulling the tote bag behind her. She loved the new suitcase. Its hard handle slid into a special compartment when not in use and she could sling the bag over her shoulder if she didn't have far to walk. Or she could pull out the straps hidden in different compartments and—*voilà*—she had a backpack. The perfect suitcase for a reporter whose next story might take her to Afghanistan, Rome or Saskatoon.

The tote bag followed effortlessly, its inline wheels soundless on the marble floor, the airline ticket snug in its outer compartment.

Was September in Paris anything like September in Montreal?

It didn't matter. She would take Paris any way it came. She would start her days with a *café au lait* and a *pain au chocolat* at a picturesque Left Bank café. Then she would shop.

She glanced down at her light slacks, cotton sweater and loafers. Good for travelling, but definitely lacking in glamour. Not to worry. With the bonus she would get from the magazine for this latest story, she'd be able to afford a little French outfit or two.

Laura pulled the suitcase to the back entrance of the building and paused at the glass door, looking around the parking lot. It was only eight o'clock on a glorious Sunday morning. She was alone.

She dug through her handbag for the remote control. Her old Honda

Civic hardly warranted an automatic starter, but she'd had enough of running out to start the car at minus twenty-five only to run back inside while it warmed up. It hadn't been easy convincing her editor to have one installed in her car. It was another reporter's tool, she had told Adam, just like a BlackBerry or a recorder. After five years of covering the seamier side of politics in Eastern Europe—not to mention getting caught in the odd civil war—she figured she deserved a perk, her recent promotion to head office notwithstanding. Adam finally gave in when she threatened to take cabs to meet her informants.

The toy was still new enough to give her a rush whenever she watched the Honda shudder to life, even with no icicles in sight.

With a sheepish glance around the empty parking lot, she pulled out the remote, pointed it at the car—parked three rows down on the far side of the lot—and pressed the start button.

She pushed open the door only to stop in shock as her car exploded in a blast that shattered windows and battered her eardrums.

Then a wave of hot air shoved the glass door closed and she stumbled back, tripped over the tote bag and landed painfully on hip and elbow.

A ball of black smoke appeared above the Honda as flames licked at the green metal paint. The car doors hung crazily off their hinges and the echo of the blast rang in her ears.

That was a bomb, she thought. *A bomb just blew up my car.*

"Shit." She bit her tongue. "Shit, shit, shit."

She stared at the remote control in her hand and controlled an impulse to fling it away from her. Finally, she stuffed it in her bag and pulled herself up. Through the heat haze of the burning car, she saw a couple of hesitant figures across the street from the parking lot. In another minute, they would pluck up enough courage to investigate.

Through the ringing in her ears, she heard faint screams coming from inside the building.

She hobbled down the mirrored hallway to the lobby, pulling the tote behind her. As she passed through the first set of entrance doors, a discreet ding announced the arrival of the elevator in the hallway behind her. She went out the front door and onto the walkway. At the sidewalk, she turned right and kept going. She didn't look back.

Five hours and three hundred and fifty miles later, she was sitting in a steamy Toronto diner, drinking bad coffee and considering her options.

She decided that her first instinct—to get out of town, fast—had been wise. She hadn't planned on going to Toronto; it happened to be the destination of the next bus leaving the Greyhound depot.

The ticket waiting in her luggage beckoned, but she ignored it. Too many people knew she was going to Paris on holiday.

So, where to go instead? Out of the country was out of the question. She might be a good reporter, but she didn't know enough about airlines to be sure she wouldn't be followed. The airport was the first place they would look.

They. Laura closed her eyes. Not they. *Him.*

Oh God.

She ran a finger around the sweaty waistband of her slacks, just to reassure herself that the pouch containing the flash drive was still there. She'd left one with the article on it on Adam's desk yesterday, but this one also contained the names of her contacts and sources. All Adam had to do was run the article.

Run the article, Adam, she prayed. *Run it, and I'll be safe.*

Once the article ran—under her byline—there would be no point to her death. In fact, her death would turn the law's thoughtful eye on Johnny Tucker. Oh no, once that article ran, Johnny T. would want her hale and hearty. But if he could prevent the article from appearing…and if she were to disappear…

She reached for her cup and spilled half of it before she managed to control her trembling.

"Here, sweetie," said the waitress, giving her an appraising look as she whisked the cup away. As if by magic, a clean cup appeared, filled with hot coffee. It smelled no better than the last one. "That one was cold anyway. Why don't you have a bite to eat? Make you feel better."

Laura looked into the woman's curious, lined eyes.

"Do you have a phone?"

The waitress blinked. Then she seemed to retreat into herself. "Sure, honey. There's a pay phone by the cash register." She finished wiping the counter and turned away. Her name tag said Annette.

"Thanks," said Laura. She went to the pay phone and placed a toll call to Adam at the magazine. Her cell phone was tucked in her desk back in Montreal because she wouldn't have been able to use it in Paris, but that was probably just as well now. She worried a cell phone would be too easy to trace.

As the coin dropped into the box, the level of tension in her stomach tightened a notch. It was just possible that Adam had betrayed her. He answered at the first ring.

"Adam Rhys," came his familiar, gruff voice, so at odds with his boyish looks.

"Adam, it's me," she said softly. The pay phone was on the wall next to the cash register, and Annette loitered nearby.

"Jesus, Laura!" said Adam, his voice breaking over her name. "Are you all right?"

"I'm fine," she said. The genuine concern in his voice flooded her with relief. Someone had betrayed her, but it wasn't Adam. He couldn't feign that level of relief. "Next time I see you, remind me to buy you a scotch for putting in that remote starter."

Adam laughed shakily. "Make it two, for scaring the crap out of me. Where are you?"

Laura hesitated. Her thinking was still muddled, but she knew enough to realize secrecy was her best defense right now. "The less you know, boss man, the better," she said, trying for flippancy. It fell flat. "Adam—do you know what happened?"

"The police are saying it was a bomb. Jesus, Laura. Why the hell didn't you stay away from the story?"

Laura sighed. That was like asking the moth why it didn't stay away from the flame. Adam had turned down the story idea when she first proposed it. If she had listened, she wouldn't be standing on the sticky floor of a diner, miles from Paris, minus one car.

She would have rested her head against the wall, but it was scribbled over with phone numbers and was dotted with splatters of what looked like dried ketchup.

"Laura, where are you?" asked Adam again. "The cops are looking for you."

"I can't tell you, Adam. For your sake as much as mine."

"But you need help!"

"Then print the story in the next issue." *Montreal Magazine* was a biweekly. The next edition was due out in a little over a week. She could stay hidden that long.

There was a long silence at the other end of the line. Finally he sighed. "Do we have an exclusive? Did you send it anywhere else?"

Laura's eyebrows rose. "Should I be insulted that you even asked?"

Adam laughed without mirth. "You were almost blown up by a bomb but you're worried about your honor?"

Laura smiled. "I wouldn't do that to you, boss. You have the exclusive." She paused. "But if it's not in the next issue, I'm sending it to the *Globe and Mail*."

"I understand, kiddo. Just be careful, okay?"

"I'll be in touch when I can. And Adam? You watch out, too."

* * *

Adam closed his cell phone and clenched it in his fist. He hadn't recognized the number—if he had, he wouldn't have answered it.

Across the table, Johnny Tucker put down his Montreal smoked meat sandwich and took a sip from his glass of Molson. Johnny always ate local. Today he had picked Schwartz's Deli instead of his favorite diner, the Paradiso. Not for him, the chain restaurants. He bought his groceries locally, too, usually at the Atwater Market, around the corner from his condo on Crescent. The only time he bought outside Montreal, or even outside Canada for that matter, was when he had to. Even then, he stuck to North America.

A patriotic crime lord, was Johnny Tucker.

"So…she checked in." Johnny patted his mouth with the oversized paper napkin. He was a wiry man with thin hair, thin lips and long grooves bracketing his mouth. He wore a light blue short-sleeved dress shirt with a tie. With his black metal-rimmed glasses and gray hair clipped short, he could have been an accountant or a businessman out for lunch with a colleague.

Except that it was Sunday, and they weren't colleagues. Not really.

The restaurant was almost full with the late lunchtime crowd. The conversations all around them formed an effective privacy barrier. And if that wasn't enough, they sat at a table in the back, by the swinging doors of the kitchen, where the clatter added to their privacy.

Adam had no doubt that Johnny's bodyguards were somewhere among the diners. When he'd walked in he thought he'd spotted Barney Hicklin's blond ponytail, but the man's face was turned away and he couldn't be sure.

Probably it wasn't Hicklin. Johnny reserved Hicklin for his dirty work. Johnny refused to walk around with thugs, as he called them.

Except for Hicklin, his bodyguards were nondescript but lethal. "A big bodyguard just attracts attention," he had once told Adam.

Adam looked down at his untouched sandwich. Acid roiled in his stomach at the thought of eating.

"Did you bring it?" asked Johnny Tucker casually.

Adam nodded and fished inside his jean pocket for the flash drive Laura had left on his desk in an envelope along with a note.

Adam, she had written, *I'm sorry I lied to you, but this was too good a story to pass up. It's all there: dates, names, scanned manifests, pictures… It's a hell of a good story. Pulitzer stuff. Just publish it in the next edition and we'll both be famous.*

I know you want to yell at me right now, but you'll have to wait until I'm back from Paris. I'm not bringing my cell phone—different systems over there.

Better start writing that acceptance speech!

—L.

He'd warned her away from the story as firmly as he could. And she'd promised she'd stay away. *Promised.* But as soon as he started reading the article, he knew he was in trouble.

If that article appeared in *Montreal Magazine*—hell, if it appeared *anywhere*—Johnny Tucker would be finished.

He'd *had* to tell Johnny about Laura's article. He'd had no choice.

He handed the flash drive to Johnny. "A bomb, Johnny?" he asked softly. "You tried to kill her?"

Johnny slipped the flash drive into his breast pocket and took another bite of the oversized sandwich. He chewed methodically, his jaw muscles bunching and releasing, all the while staring at Adam. Pale blue eyes, Adam realized. In all the years he'd known Johnny Tucker, he'd never noticed that before.

"A bit of an overreaction," agreed Johnny after a swallow of beer.

His tongue fished around his teeth, extracting bits of meat.

Adam almost rolled his eyes but didn't. He'd known Johnny since he was a reporter on the Port beat. Johnny had been his source on a lot of the illegal activities that were taking place there. It was only after Johnny was named Director of Customs at the Montreal Port Authority that Adam looked back and realized he had helped Johnny get rid of all his rivals. By then, it was too late. Johnny Tucker had become a powerful figure in the Montreal underworld.

And Adam was responsible for getting him there.

In his more honest moments, he acknowledged that he'd gained a lot from their relationship. He'd made editor at the magazine on the basis of stories he'd filed about the Port—stories he'd been fed by Johnny Tucker.

So when he heard something that would affect Johnny—as when his sources told him the cops had planned a sting operation at the Port—well, it only seemed fair that he warn Johnny.

Especially when Johnny's gratitude came in the form of unmarked bills. The money had been a godsend, helping him pay for his mother to go to the States for expensive experimental cancer treatment and then place her in the very best care facility in Montreal. It had taken three years for the cancer to finally take her.

He brought himself back to the present. "The problem is that the cops have been asking me questions."

"What kind of questions?" asked Johnny around another mouthful of meat.

What kind of questions? What the hell did he *think* they were asking? "Does Laura have any enemies? Would anyone have any reason to want her dead? What story was she working on? You know." He was very careful to keep his tone respectful.

Too many disrespectful people had disappeared around Johnny

Tucker lately. It was a new development. Adam had never known Johnny to resort to violence before. Maybe he wasn't very good at it, judging by the car bomb.

"Hmm." Johnny finally pushed his plate away. In the past few years, he'd developed a little paunch. He was forty-nine, but he looked closer to sixty-three.

Must be the stress of the job, thought Adam.

"Where is she?" asked Johnny quietly.

Careful, Adam warned himself. He looked at Johnny. "I don't know. She refused to tell me."

A waiter stopped at their table and swept up Johnny's plate and cutlery and, at Adam's nod, his untouched food. As soon as he was out of earshot, Johnny leaned forward.

"You need to find her, Adam."

Adam felt himself flushing hot. The words tumbled out of him before he could hold them back. "Why? So you can finish the job you started?"

Johnny's eyebrows rose in surprise. "You like this girl?"

Adam struggled for composure, clamping his damp hands on his knees beneath the table. "Yes, I like her, Johnny. I've worked with her for a lot of years."

Johnny sat back in his chair and studied Adam. Finally he raised his glass and drank the last of the beer before setting it down.

"All right, Adam. Because of our long friendship, I'll give you a chance to save her." He leaned forward and set his elbows on the tablecloth. "You find her. Talk to her. Get her to come back here so *I* can talk to her. If you can both convince me she'll keep her mouth shut, she'll be safe." He took a deep breath. "But if she won't, I may have to do something you'll both regret."

The blood drained from Adam's face, leaving him suddenly cold—

whether with fear, or anger, he couldn't tell. "Are you threatening me, Johnny?"

Johnny Tucker looked genuinely hurt. "I don't have to threaten you, Adam. You're smart enough to realize that if I go down, you go down. You have to keep her quiet, for both our sakes. Find her, Adam. We're running out of time."

CHAPTER TWO

The rig came to a stop in a series of gasps and exhales. Laura shook herself awake, momentarily disoriented.

"This is where I turn off," said Bert. His eyes crinkled in sympathy as he watched her. He waited patiently, his big hands resting on the steering wheel. A picture of his wife and ten-year-old daughter was clipped to the visor, where he could see it every time he glanced up.

Laura blinked hard, willing herself to alertness. The Skagway turnoff. She looked around. There was the gas station with its attached diner. It had a new paint job. A few pickup trucks were parked in front of it. It was too early for the lunch crowd, too late for the morning rush. A car passed them, heading south on the Alaska Highway. *Tourist season is over,* thought Laura, *or there'd be a lot more traffic.*

"Thanks, Bert. I appreciate the ride." She tugged on the door handle with one hand and hooked her suitcase strap with the other. "You're a prince among men."

The truck driver rolled his eyes and grinned, waving her off.

Laura meant it. Five rides in long-haul rigs and she was now a fan of truckers. Toronto to Winnipeg, then Edmonton, Fort St. John, Watson Lake and finally Whitehorse. In spite of the distance and the uncertainty of her next ride, it had taken less than five days to drive the almost 3,500 miles to her childhood home.

If she got out of this mess alive, she would write a story about truck drivers.

Laura slid down to the step just below the passenger door, then hopped down, holding the suitcase away from her so it wouldn't bang against her or trip her on landing. She swung the door closed and waved as Bert pulled away from the shoulder, the rig rumbling as he shifted gears. He turned onto the secondary highway toward Skagway and finally disappeared over the rise.

She turned back to the Alaska Highway, bag in hand, and stared down its lonely length. Exhaustion caught at her throat, threatening release as a sob, but she couldn't afford to go to pieces yet. She was still four miles from her mother's house, four miles she would have to cover on foot.

With a groan she hauled the straps over her shoulders and shrugged the backpack into place. She no longer loved it. It was a poor suitcase and a worse backpack.

She glanced longingly at the gas station behind her. It would be so easy to walk over, plop a quarter in the pay phone and call home. "Come get me," she would say, as if she were a teenager at a party. "I'm tired."

She wished she could call Jason, but he was working in Vancouver for one of the daily newspapers. Maybe his dad would come. Mr. Howell had always been fond of her.

But she couldn't call anyone. Somebody at the gas station might recognize her. As long as she remained another hitchhiker seen from a distance, no one would pay attention to her. And it wasn't fair to involve Mr. Howell if she wasn't willing to give his paper the story.

She sighed.

One mile later, she turned off the highway onto Wild Rose Lane. Almost three miles to go—two and a half on the dirt road before she finally reached her mother's long driveway.

At the top of the lane, she paused. She had grown up on Wild Rose Lane, which wasn't a lane, really. It was a well-graded, hard-packed road with a dozen smaller roads branching off it. Each one led to one or more homes sitting on a parcel of forty acres of land. If she stayed on the road, a neighbor was bound to drive by.

With another sigh she climbed into and out of the dry ditch and entered the sparse woods.

* * *

Fay stopped the car in front of the house and switched off the engine. Hefting a grocery bag in each arm, she pushed the car door shut with her hip and walked around to the back of the house. She left the groceries and her purse on the back porch, then headed for the garden.

The fenced garden crowned the cliff where it began to slope upward. Some romaine lettuce had survived the first frosts and the cauliflower and broccoli were thriving. Another week and the brussels sprouts would be ready for harvesting.

As always, the garden worked its soothing magic on her. She wandered through the herb beds, taking deep breaths, allowing the accumulated pain of other women to slip away from her. No misery was allowed in this garden. No ghosts, either.

The river flowed a hundred feet below the garden, though she couldn't see it from her vantage point. Across the ravine, the forest picked up where it had left off, trees marching in green and yellow splendor, ridge upon ridge, until the colors faded into the purple distance.

She glanced up at the cloudless sky. Frost tonight, no doubt. She would bring in the last of the garden flowers. They might as well grace her table for a few days before dying.

She had already harvested the carrots and the potatoes, which were safely stored in the cold room. Judging by the size of the broccoli, however, it would be the vegetable of choice for dinner tonight. Fresh broccoli, steamed and tossed in hot olive oil and garlic. Yum. Her stomach growled in anticipation.

As she strolled between the beds, she gradually became aware that she was being watched. Her smile faded. James or Sawyer? Or both? Reluctantly she turned toward the house.

Laura stood on the back porch, tall and pale, and Fay's heart lurched.

"Hi, Fay," said Laura.

Relief settled in the pit of her stomach. Not dead, then. Not a ghost.

"Laura," she finally managed to say. "What's the matter? Why aren't you in Paris?"

Her daughter's expression closed down.

There, I've done it again, thought Fay.

"I'm glad to see you, too, Fay," said Laura.

The smile she gave her mother was half rueful, half bitter, and Fay wanted to call a time out. *Let's try again,* she wanted to say. *I can do better.*

Instead she sighed. "Come inside. You must be hungry."

* * *

"But can't you go to the police here?" asked Fay. She stood on the other side of the work island from Laura, her hands poised over the salad bowl. A piece of torn romaine lettuce drooped from one hand.

Laura continued arranging garden flowers in a shallow vase. She concentrated on stripping excess leaves from the marigolds before tucking them in among the others. Fay watched her expectantly.

Finally Laura shrugged. "I could go to the police, but even if they're all made of sterling stuff, someone will get careless. A report will land on the wrong desk. A phone conversation will be overheard. That's how

I get a lot of *my* information. But once the magazine comes out, I'll be safe, no matter who's on Mr. T.'s payroll."

Above the sink the ruffled yellow curtains billowed out. In the growing darkness beyond the open window, the trees swaying in the wind were visible only as shadowy movements. A single lamp glowed in the living room below the kitchen railing, an island of light in a pool of night. She had forgotten how quickly night fell in the North at this time of year.

"Is he really that dangerous?" asked Fay.

Laura nodded cautiously. Clearly Fay hadn't heard about the explosion and there was no point in telling her about it. At least, not right away. Fay didn't have a television and had never felt the need to keep up with the news. By the time she finally did learn about the explosion, Johnny T. would already be in jail.

The explosion had taught her caution. Johnny Tucker was powerful. That he would try to kill a reporter so publicly meant he was sure of himself and his police contacts. It also meant she couldn't trust anyone.

His strength was his anonymity. Few people knew what Johnny Tucker did when he left his Port Customs office at five o'clock every day. As Director, he was aware of all shipped merchandise coming into the Port of Montreal. At first, he'd merely falsified a document here or delayed a shipment there. Now he controlled drug smuggling on the east coast and was expanding to the west coast.

She had only found him because she knew he must exist. From the day she arrived in Montreal, the rival biker gangs vying for control of drug smuggling on Montreal's docks had fascinated her. Then she met a business reporter at an economics conference in Vancouver. Over drinks one night the reporter told Laura about the resurgence of Asian gang wars in Vancouver's port. They both agreed the real money wasn't at the gang level.

Something inside Laura had clicked. Montreal police were busy trying to control gang warfare on the docks. And according to the Vancouver reporter, that city's finest were trying to keep Asian gangs from each other's throats… which meant the police had few resources left to deal with smuggling.

Laura had tried to convince Adam there was a story behind the gang warfare, but he turned her down.

"We did a biker story just two months ago," he'd said, leaning back in his chair and twirling his pen between his palms. He quirked an eyebrow at her. "What about the flooding in Chambly? I've heard complaints that the new drainage system is under-spec. Have you spoken to any city officials yet?"

In the five years she had known Adam Rhys, she had come to recognize that particular look in his eye, the look that said, *This discussion is over.*

So she'd pursued it on her own time. Two months and some serious digging later, she found Johnny Tucker. She had traced Swiss bank accounts, spied on his secret meetings, bribed accountants. The man was worth millions, yet none of her regular contacts knew of his existence. She was willing to bet that if anyone in the biker gangs knew, it was at the higher echelons only.

But she couldn't tell Fay any of it. It was bad enough that her mother knew the story existed.

"And the magazine is due out when?" asked Fay.

"On Wednesday." In two days she would be safe.

Fay stared at her daughter, digesting the information. After a while she turned her attention back to the bowl and resumed tearing the lettuce.

Laura stole a glance at her mother's reflection in the balcony door window. There was a lot of silver in Fay's short, blond hair, but she didn't look fifty-three. Her eyes were still the startling blue that Laura had always envied. She carried herself well, her back straight, her head high, so that Laura always forgot Fay was four inches shorter than her. Working hard, walking and skiing kept her slim.

Laura relaxed. Fay wouldn't press. She hadn't even asked the obvious—why not leave copies of the story with several people and let it be known that she had done so?

Laura had considered it, but she worried it would endanger those she involved. It would also multiply the chances of a rival obtaining a copy of her story, robbing her of her scoop. So she had compromised. She'd placed three notarized and sealed copies of the article with three courier companies. Two days after the magazine appeared on the newsstands, the envelopes were to be delivered to the federal Crown Attorney's office, to RCMP headquarters in Regina and to the business reporter in Vancouver who had unknowingly given her the tip.

She didn't tell Adam. Not only had she disobeyed him, she had robbed the magazine of its exclusive rights to her work. She was gambling that once Adam published it—and he would, he had promised—the magazine wouldn't fire the reporter who had written the story of the decade. It would make her reputation as a reporter and was worth some risk.

But who else was she willing to risk?

Laura realized she was crushing the marigolds.

This was a mistake, she decided abruptly. She should never have come here. No matter how unlikely, there was still a chance she would be found within the next two days. She should never have exposed Fay to danger, especially when Fay didn't know how serious the danger was.

"I'll go in the morning, Fay," she said, and realized how blunt it sounded as soon as Fay raised her head.

She knew her mother didn't like it when Laura called her by her given name. She didn't know why she kept it up—habit more than anything else. Besides, she'd never been a touchy-feely kind of daughter.

"What I meant," Laura added, "is that I should never have exposed you to this. I don't know what I was thinking."

Fay smiled. "You did what anyone would have done. You headed for the one place you always felt safe."

Laura looked at her mother, unable to speak. Home had been safe as long as Dad was alive. Why had she come here? Had she honestly hoped she would be safe?

"Fay…" she began.

"No," said Fay, putting up a hand. "Where would you go? The magazine is out in two days," she added calmly. "Stay at least that long. Then we can discuss it."

CHAPTER THREE

In the morning Laura waited for her mother to leave for work before getting up. Fay now worked two days a week at a women's safe house, but hadn't said why. The *why* was clear to Laura. Her parents had had a strained marriage. Now that her husband was dead, Fay wanted to help women whose relationships had gone beyond strained. But Laura couldn't help thinking Fay's choice of work was like advertising her marital difficulties to the whole world, and an implicit criticism of Dad.

Her first impulse on rising was to see the river. She padded barefoot to the kitchen balcony and stood in her nightgown, shivering and rubbing her arms. Below her the river rumbled in steely glory. The sun peeked over the mountain range and frost sparkled like magic dust on the garden. The shadows on the cliffs opposite seemed cool and mysterious. Wilted fireweed had turned from fiery red to rust, brown and yellow, and spiky foxtail seeds cartwheeled through the air, waiting to hook on fur, feather or fabric.

Laura went back inside and took a hot shower. The house needed no tidying. Her mother's room, at the other end of the house from hers, was neat. A new bedspread graced the bed, matching the new curtains. The geometric pattern with its mustard yellow accents contrasted well with the green walls. Nothing else had changed in the house.

Five years earlier, Dad had converted the second-floor guest bedroom to a workroom for Fay's quilting. A large cutting table filled one side of the room. The wall above it was fitted with a pegboard from which hung various scissors and rolling blades, measuring tapes, gridded cutting boards and clear plastic rulers for cutting even strips of fabric. Against the opposite wall, beneath the window, Fay had set up her sewing machine. Another pegboard, about four feet by four feet, was screwed to the wall, next to the machine. It was filled with multi-colored bobbins of thread, a cheerful mosaic. A quilt stand in one corner held three folded quilts in various stages of completion. An ironing board hung neatly on its holder behind the door, the iron safely stored in its own compartment.

Laura left the sewing room and went to the room next to it. It had been designed as a music room but was rarely used as one. Open to the rest of the house, it faced the equally open kitchen across from, and looking down on, the sunken living room. A series of long, narrow windows on the upper level filled the house with light and gave the music room the best light in the house. There Fay had set up her quilting loom. Laura wandered over to the quilt in progress, admiring the tones of amethyst, rose and emerald that formed the main colors of the work. Flying Clouds, thought Laura, recognizing the pattern. Beautiful.

The telephone rang, giving her a start. She waited, controlling the impulse that almost sent her running for the kitchen extension. One, two, three, four rings. Finally the answering machine clicked on.

"You've reached 555-7344 and I can't come to the phone right now," said her mother's voice. "Please leave a message at the sound of the tone."

The tone came on and Laura waited, but only silence followed. After five seconds, the caller hung up.

Not her mother, then. They had agreed Fay would leave a message on the machine to identify herself. Only then would Laura pick up.

Disturbed, Laura returned to the kitchen. She shouldn't let the anonymous caller bother her. Lots of people refused to leave messages on answering machines.

In the freezer she found a package of stewing meat, and that decided her. An hour and a half later, the stew was slowly simmering in the crock pot. She made herself a cheese and tomato sandwich and sat on the balcony to eat it.

The sun warmed the balcony and Laura stripped off her sweatshirt. It was definitely T-shirt weather, too beautiful to be inside. She finished her sandwich and went back in. Once her dishes were washed, she rummaged around the front entrance cupboard, finally pulling out an old fanny pack to carry a plastic bottle full of juice. She added a book of matches that she found in the drawer next to the stove and snapped the pack around her waist. With the bottle bumping against her lower back, she ran down the stairs, walked through the living room and past her father's study. The sense of his presence was so strong that she had to force herself out the door.

She strolled toward the cliff trail, heading upslope. Cool air bathed her face with moisture and her skin drank it in thirstily. Her hands already looked like snake skin thanks to the dry climate. Then she reached the crest of the hill and forgot all about dry skin. The Yukon River tumbled far below her, roaring its way to Whitehorse.

A trail of sorts led from the top of the cliff to the river, almost a hundred feet down. If she looked carefully, she could see the remains of the dock she and her father had built almost two decades ago. They had kept a dinghy with a small motor. On lazy summer weekends she and Dad used to float downriver almost to the Takhini River, then putter back upstream to a worried Fay, long past supper time. Or sometimes Fay would meet them with the truck at Takhini Landing and they would put the craft on the trailer and drive back.

She eyed the trail dubiously and decided she was no longer a nimble twelve-year-old. It would be too ironic if she escaped Johnny Tucker's long reach only to kill herself falling down a cliff.

As she stood admiring the view, she suddenly remembered how frightened Fay was of heights. Her mother could never bring herself to come close to the cliff's edge, let alone climb down the trail to join them in the dinghy. Funny that she should live here all these years, so close to what she feared most.

Laura moved on, dividing her attention between the path and the view. After days of being cooped up in noisy, smelly long-haul rigs, it felt wonderful to breathe fresh air and hear nothing more than the occasional raven squawking or red squirrel chattering at her. Her stride lengthened as she stretched her legs and took deep breaths. In spite of everything, and for the moment, she was happy.

Ten minutes later she spotted another trail branching off the cliff path and hesitated. This trail led to the old cabin. She hadn't thought of it in years—and hadn't visited it in at least ten years. For as long as she could remember, the cabin had sat on their land, empty. Her parents didn't allow her to play there, but she and her friends hadn't been able to resist the lure of an abandoned cabin.

Feeling a bit like a disobedient teenager, Laura left the cliff path and headed deeper into the forest of pine and poplar. A gust of wind dropped a swirl of yellow poplar leaves onto the path ahead of her.

Moments later she spotted the dilapidated mass. It was even smaller than she remembered. The line of the roof was still intact, and the walls were still straight, but otherwise it was in sad shape. The chinks in the log walls had fallen out and the sod roof had been dead for as long as she could remember, its long grasses and weeds dried to a tangle of stalks that overhung the door and windows. Over the years, wind storms had flung branches at the windows, breaking most of the panes. Fireweed and delphinium grew high against the cabin walls. The cabin sat in a pocket of darkness, as if it swallowed light and breathed out sadness.

With a shake of her head she approached the door, taking care to test each step on the rotting wooden porch. The steps were solid enough but the railing wobbled under her hand.

Why hadn't her parents kept the cabin up? It had good bones—it would have made a great rental property. Close enough to Whitehorse to drive to work, yet far enough to forget about town every night. Her father, especially, always had an eye for a good investment. But neither he nor Fay had ever wanted to discuss the cabin.

She opened the door, wincing as the rusted hinges protested loudly. Despite the broken windows, the inside of the cabin smelled musty. In a moment her eyes adjusted to the dimness. Disturbed by her footsteps, dust rose through the thin rays of light. A narrow ladder leaned against the loft, where an old mattress waited. Squirrels and other rodents had made a mess of the stuffing.

Smiling, she left the cabin. She and her girlfriends used to pretend it was the cabin of an old miner who never came back because a bear had gotten him, or because he'd been bushwhacked by bad guys, or had tumbled off the cliff and drowned or fallen down a gully and died because no one could hear his screams.

They used to scare each other with the possibility of his return… and the possible *state* of his return.

As she walked away, a furtive movement caught her eye. She paused, stilled by the sudden recollection that this was bear country. But the eyes that stared back at her from the bushes thirty yards away were sly and knowing. They blinked at her and the fox turned, disappearing into the dappled bushes. Laura caught a glimpse of reddish gold fur before it became just another shadow.

The aroma of simmering stew greeted her when she approached the house. Then she opened the door to the sound of a man singing.

Her heart skipped a beat and she stood in the doorway for a long moment, poised between the need to know and the urge to flee. Had she been discovered? By a singing bad guy?

She stepped into the house, trying to localize the singing. Then she had it—the shower. A man was singing, off key, in her mother's shower.

What the hell was going on?

Laura stood in the middle of the sunny hallway, at a loss. It didn't seem likely that anyone looking for her would pause to take a shower in her mother's house. Still, someone was definitely in the shower, someone Fay hadn't expected or she would have warned Laura.

She couldn't go charging into the bathroom and demand to know what the naked man was doing here. Then again, he would be at a disadvantage… With a sigh she decided on discretion.

She could leave the way she had come. But that would mean a stranger—maybe a friend of her mother's, but maybe not—would have free access to the house. What if he stole something? On the other hand, why would a thief stop to take a shower?

What if he stayed? She wasn't prepared to wait outside until Fay came home to introduce him. She quietly closed the door behind her, shutting herself in with the stranger.

She was alone in the house with a strange man—probably not, all things considered, one of Johnny Tucker's executioners, but still, a stranger. It would be nice to have some kind of protection, just in case. Her father had kept a baseball bat in the cupboard in the entrance hall. It was just the spine stiffener she needed. Once she had the baseball bat, it was only a few quick steps to her bedroom, where she would be out of sight. Unfortunately, she had to cross the living room to get the bat, which would put her in plain view of the main floor bathroom, from which issued the off-key baritone.

The door to the bathroom remained closed. If she hurried…

Without giving herself a chance to change her mind, she stepped down onto the hardwood floor of the sunken living room.

The shower stopped and the door to the bathroom opened, catching her in mid-tiptoe. She stared in amazement as a great cloud of steam billowed out of the bathroom. When it finally settled, she saw she still had a chance. The man had opened the door to clear the air. He now stood with his back to her, humming and lathering a shaving brush with soap. He was quite naked.

She squelched the part of her that wanted to giggle hysterically and resumed her stealthy advance through the living room, crouching as low as possible.

"Hey!" called the man, whipping around. "What the hell…?" He tried to tie a towel around his waist while still holding onto the shaving brush.

With as much dignity as she could muster, Laura straightened from her crouch and turned to face the stranger.

Her first impression was of size—wide, heavy shoulders, muscled arms and a trim belly. A line of damp, dark hair led from his belly button and disappeared beneath the towel. Her face flamed with embarrassment, and she didn't dare look lower. His thick, dark hair was slicked back from the shower and his cheeks were dark with stubble. His blue eyes were so dark they looked navy. They weren't smiling.

Having successfully tied the towel around his waist, the man tossed the shaving brush into the sink and stepped out of the washroom. He seemed to fill the doorway, and she swallowed hard. Once he no longer blocked her view, Laura saw herself reflected in the mirror. It still bore the traces of his quick wipe.

Fighting an illogical sense of guilt, Laura kept quiet and watched. *Let him talk first,* she decided. Always a good tactical move.

"Who the hell are you?" he demanded. "And what are you doing in Fay's house?" There was no force behind his words. He stared at her with an odd expression, as if…

"Aha!" he cried, lifting a finger to point at her. "Wait right there!" Still clutching the towel around his waist, he stalked to her room, only to return a moment later with a framed picture in his hand.

"You're Laura," he said accusingly and turned the photo toward her. "You're Fay's daughter."

Laura stared at her college graduation picture and sighed. So much for secrecy.

"I'm Fay's daughter." She pointed at the room he had so casually entered. "And that's my room. You, on the other hand, are a mostly naked man in my mother's house. Which do you think needs more explaining?"

Under her steady gaze, he hesitated. He glanced down at her picture, then at the puddles his wet feet had left on the hardwood floor. Finally he looked at the towel wrapped around his middle. A dark flush started somewhere in the region of his chest and climbed quickly to his hairline.

"Give me a minute to get dressed," he said.

Laura nodded and he went into the bathroom, closing the door behind him. She stared at it for a moment, suddenly unsure of her legs. She was in deep trouble. The last thing she needed was a wild card in the deck. Somehow she had to convince this man to keep quiet about her.

* * *

28

Mack dressed quickly and finished shaving without cutting himself. She was older than she was in the picture, of course, and much more attractive. The photographer hadn't captured the strength in her face or the sensuality in the curve of her lips. He stuffed the towel and his dirty clothes into his backpack and stepped into the hallway. She wasn't there. Then he noticed the puddles he had left on Fay's floor and pulled the towel out of his backpack again.

Finally he climbed the stairs by twos and tossed the backpack into the corner of the kitchen. Laura was on the balcony, her back to him. The sun glinted off her shoulder-length hair, bringing out the auburn in it. She had made coffee, and he helped himself to a cup, using the moment to study her.

She was tall and lean, her jeans a bit too big in the butt for her. Long legs, wide shoulders. He wondered if she was a swimmer.

Fay hadn't known Laura was coming, or she would have said something. Was there a problem? The woman had been skulking around as if she didn't want to be seen. And why hadn't she just waited until he came out of the shower to introduce herself, like a normal person?

Because he was buck naked, for one thing. And a stranger to her.

Mack almost groaned. It was one of Fay's work days. Despite the smell of the stew, which he'd thought was in a crock pot, he had—reasonably, he thought—assumed he was alone in the house. What a way to meet the woman he'd been hearing so much about all summer.

Well, don't just stand there like an idiot, he told himself. *Go talk to her!*

Laura turned to face him as he opened the door. Her face was carefully neutral.

What is she thinking? he wondered.

"Hi," he said, stepping closer. He put his hand out. "I'm Mack Hawkins."

She shook his hand firmly. Her hand was warm and strong, and he found himself reluctant to release it. Finally she slid it out of his grasp, her color high.

"I'm…"

"Laura May Thorsen," he said wryly, ignoring her wince at the use of her middle name, "star reporter for *Montreal Magazine*." He smiled at her raised eyebrows. "Your mother made me read everything you've ever written, including a couple of high school essays."

She blushed, looking confused, and he wondered why that surprised her. Surely it was normal for Fay to brag about her successful reporter daughter?

"I hadn't realized Fay had kept my essays." Her voice was low, and he tried to imagine how she sounded when she laughed.

She called her mother by her given name?

"Relax," said Mack. "I didn't mind—you're a good reporter, and a better writer."

An expression crossed her face, so fleeting that he wondered if he had imagined it. Why would his words cause her pain?

"Mr. Hawkins," she said, "what are you doing here?"

For the first time, it occurred to him that Fay hadn't told her about him.

"I room here," he finally answered. "Or at least I did. I'm surprised she didn't tell you."

"You room here," repeated Laura.

He watched her, fascinated. He could almost read her thoughts, just from watching the expressions chase each other on her face. She was wondering if Fay needed the money, or—horrors!—if there was something between him and her mother. She eyed him warily, obviously trying to judge his age.

I'm thirty-six, he wanted to say, but doubted that would help her.

"I…uh," she faltered.

He took pity on her. "I'm your neighbor," he said. "I'm building a house. Instead of driving in from town every day or living in a tent while it was under construction, Fay let me board here."

Ah, relief.

"You finished your house?"

Then why were you in my mother's shower? finished Mack silently. "I've moved into the basement of my house—it's finished enough for that. But I still don't have running water, which is why Fay lets me shower here."

"Oh," said Laura. Then she stopped and looked at him. "Um, which room…?"

"Your room," he said quietly. "It's closest to the door."

In the sudden, awkward silence, they stared at each other. Finally Laura stirred.

"Do you like stew?"

* * *

When Fay arrived home, she decided to skip her usual garden visit. It was beginning to look exhausted, and its spent promise now saddened her. Besides, Laura was waiting.

She opened the door and stopped, staring at the handle. It wasn't locked. Of course it wasn't locked. She never locked it. She would have to remind Laura to keep it locked.

She pushed the door open and entered. An enticing smell and the sound of Laura's laughter reached her at the same time. Smiling, Fay placed the carton of milk on the deacon's bench and shrugged out of her jacket. She picked up the milk and was about to call out to Laura when a man laughed.

Holding her breath, Fay stepped into the doorway and looked up the stairs into the open kitchen to find the source of the laughter.

Time bent itself, and suddenly she saw herself at nineteen, standing in the unfinished kitchen, laughing up at Sawyer as she handed him a sandwich on a plate.

The milk carton slipped from her grasp and landed with a thud at her feet. Fay blinked down at it.

"Fay?"

Fay slowly looked up. Laura stood at the top of the stairs, frowning in concern. She held a cutting board on which rested a miniature loaf of bread.

"Fay, are you all right?" asked Mack. He stood next to Laura, an old wool shirt hanging outside his favorite blue jeans.

Relief threatened to rob her legs of strength. Mack, not Sawyer.

"Yes, of course I'm fine," she replied, with only a faint tremolo in her voice. She smiled at him.

Then, as if drawn by an invisible magnet, she looked beyond Mack, to where James stood insubstantially before the kitchen balcony door.

"Oh, my dear God," she whispered. He had never come inside the house before.

Something in her face alarmed Laura and Mack. He ran down the stairs and took her arm, helping her down the one step into the living room and into the recliner by the window. She knew he was aware of her trembling, but couldn't stop herself. Before she sank into the welcoming arms of the chair, she glanced up at the kitchen.

Gone.

Then Laura was by her side, pressing a glass of water into her hands.

"Drink," ordered her daughter, and she obediently drank.

"Thank you, dear," she said, clearing her throat when the words caught. "I'm fine, really." She placed the glass on the telephone table next to the recliner and made to get up.

"Sure you are," said Mack gently, forcing her back down. "But humor us."

Fay couldn't help but smile at him. He really was a nice young man. She glanced from one concerned face to another. Yes, he was a nice, young, *unmarried* man.

"What was that all about?" demanded Laura. As usual, concern sharpened her tone, making her sound angry.

"Just a dizzy spell," lied Fay. "I didn't have lunch today."

Laura frowned and even Mack seemed ready to dispute her excuse.

She couldn't tell them the truth—especially when she didn't know what the truth was. Something had changed in the haunting. In the three months James and Sawyer had been haunting her, neither one had ever come into the house, as if by unspoken agreement. If not for the fact that she was losing her mind, it would be funny. That these two should agree in death when they had never agreed in life…

The sudden ringing of the telephone shattered the tense silence. She jumped and reached for it but Mack picked it up before she could.

"Hello?" he said into the mouthpiece. Then he looked at Laura. "Laura?"

Laura paled and shook her head violently. Fay stood up and went to stand by her daughter, shaking her head at him, too.

"Sorry," said Mack politely, still looking at Laura, "you must have the wrong number." He hung up quietly. The three of them stood in tableau for a few seconds, then Mack smiled.

"If I'm going to lie for you, the least you can do is tell me why."

CHAPTER FOUR

Fay set the coffee cup down harder than necessary. The clock on the stove read five after nine, well past time to get up. Her restless gaze settled on the downstairs bedroom door, which remained resolutely shut. Laura was thirty-three years old—hadn't she outgrown that teenage slothfulness yet?

She rubbed her face, trying to massage herself into wakefulness. Who had called for Laura last night? The look on Laura's face when she realized someone was asking for her…

With a sigh Fay pushed her chair back, took her empty cup to the sink and rinsed it. She placed it on the drain board to keep company with her breakfast dishes and stared out the window above the sink. As if to spite the sun warming her face, the wind sent a volley of aspen leaves tumbling to the ground.

She wished Laura would get up.

James hadn't been a morning person, either. He had slept as if drugged, and struggled every morning for wakefulness. Even when Laura was a baby, he had never been able to awaken enough to help during the night. He had worked hard during those early years, setting up a solid foundation for his accounting firm. The strain had shown in his nightmares, from which he would awaken with a shout, drenched in sweat. She had tried not to begrudge him his sleep, even as she dragged herself through her exhausted days.

And if, late at night, her thoughts turned to Sawyer, she never let her sadness show during the day. Sawyer had gone, and James had stayed.

Over the years, especially that first year, she found herself wondering more than once if James had said something to Sawyer to make him go. James always refused to discuss it, even though sometimes he shouted out Sawyer's name in his restless sleep.

"Good morning."

Fay jumped, her hand going to her throat. She turned around.

Laura stood at the top of the stairs, barefoot in an old gray sweat suit salvaged from the back of her closet.

"Sorry, Fay." Her daughter grinned. "I didn't mean to startle you."

Fay. When Laura had turned twelve, she took to calling her Fay instead of Mom. Fay should have stopped it right at beginning, but James teased her about it, telling her it was just a phase Laura was going through. Funny how she had become Fay while James always remained Dad.

Fay tried to grin back. "You don't look sorry at all."

Laura raked her fingers through snarled shoulder-length hair. Her face still wore pillow creases and there were dark circles under her green eyes.

Fay immediately regretted her impatience. Of course Laura hadn't slept well—she was worried about that Johnny T.

That made two of them.

"Would you like some coffee?" she asked, picking up the coffee pot.

"Sure." Laura went to the cupboard for a cup and held it out for Fay to fill. "You don't work today?"

Fay shook her head. "Only Mondays and Tuesdays." She followed her daughter to the table and sat down.

Laura took a deep breath. "Why?"

"Why only two days? Well…"

"No, why work there at all? Why do you want to work in such a depressing environment?"

Fay studied her daughter, trying to gauge how much of the censure in her tone came from worry, and how much from disapproval. But why would she disapprove? *Careful,* she told herself. *This one's a minefield.*

"I work there because I make a difference. I was trained as a nurse, you know. Some of those women come in pretty battered and don't want to go to the hospital."

"Jesus, Fay." Laura's eyes narrowed and Fay braced herself. "I know they need help, but that's not the place for you."

"It doesn't happen every day, and it's good to feel useful again," said Fay as calmly as she could. "It's really not as bad as you think."

"What was last night all about then?" asked Laura. "I've never known you to faint."

"I did not faint!"

"Just about!" said Laura, frowning over her coffee cup. "You deal with women and children who have been beaten up. That job is too stressful. You should quit. At least see a doctor."

Fay bristled. Laura was a fine one to talk about stressful jobs. At least Fay didn't have underworld killers chasing her.

And after weeks of no contact, Laura's sudden concern rankled. She had called at least once a week while James was alive, no matter which part of the world she was in. Now Fay was lucky if she spoke to her daughter once a month.

"Why the sudden interest, Laura?" she asked, unable—unwilling— to disguise the bitterness in her voice. "I can't remember the last time you called."

"You know I've been busy!" Laura no longer looked sleepy. "And you could have called me!"

"I'm sick of talking to your voicemail," replied Fay tiredly. *And I'm sick of you turning your back on me.*

She had tried. After James's funeral, she had gone to Montreal with Laura for a week, but her daughter had been too busy with work to spend much time with her. What time they did spend together was strained. They had spoken exactly twice since then.

Fay got up. "I'm sure you can get your own breakfast."

She went into her workroom and closed the door. So much for minefields. She'd just driven a tank across this one. After a few minutes she heard Laura go downstairs and take a shower. She looked at the square she was pinning and realized she had pinned one of the triangles wrong side up. With a sigh, she took the pins out and dropped the triangles back in the basket.

She suspected that Laura saw her working in a safe house as an indictment of her marriage to James. She had heard the disapproval in her daughter's voice when she found out. But it had nothing to do with James. She was now doing things for herself, not in relationship to a husband or a child.

She leaned her forehead against the cool metal of the sewing machine and closed her eyes. She had thought she would dream of Laura last night, but her dreams had been full of James's sadness, of Sawyer's loving eyes, of echoing anguish.

Would she never be free? Why did the past cling to her when Sawyer himself had cut their ties?

Were these two men, once friends, truly haunting her? Or were they conjured out of a guilt too long ignored?

She could understand James haunting her, but Sawyer? Not once had she seen him or heard from him in the thirty-four years since his disappearance. No one outside the Yukon had come looking for him or asked about him. She had reported him missing, but the police had assumed he'd left town on his own. And with James standing right there, she couldn't tell them she and Sawyer were supposed to run away together.

What if he had changed his mind?

After a while she convinced herself Sawyer had stolen away in the night. It was much later that suspicion entered her heart.

James never talked about Sawyer or went near Sawyer's cabin. He refused to rent it out, refused to even discuss it with her.

Did he know something about Sawyer's disappearance? Had he suspected she and Sawyer were lovers? The questions always remained, even after more than thirty years of marriage. She had never worked up the courage to ask them.

At least now she knew for sure Sawyer *was* dead. But why had James's death triggered Sawyer's appearance? Were they to be forever linked, she and the two loves of her life?

Her daughter needed her. She couldn't waste time on two dead men. Maybe Laura was right. Maybe she should see a doctor.

Or maybe, instead of snapping at her daughter, she should confide in her.

* * *

Laura briskly toweled her hair and then straightened, flipping the wet strands back. Standing in front of the dresser mirror, she tugged at the tangle with a comb and tried to figure out how she had upset her mother.

It was true that she had been busier than usual lately, but that was a reporter's life. Fay had never objected before. But Dad had been around before. Maybe he had been enough for her.

39

For over three months, Laura had been preoccupied with the loss of her father, and not preoccupied enough with her mother's loss of her husband.

With painful clarity she realized she didn't know how her mother was feeling. Was Fay lonely? Had her self-sufficient, distant mother actually missed her?

She suddenly felt as confused and uncertain as she had yesterday when Mack told her Fay had saved all her articles and school work.

At the thought of Mack, Laura turned to stare at the mussed up quilt on the bed, remembering last night and how she had felt when she first realized that he had slept in her bed.

Her night had been plagued by erotic dreams of Mack, with a dark dose of nightmares mixed in. Johnny Tucker chased her through a field of flash drives, on a mechanical horse, his eyes flashing alternately red and green, a mad electronic jockey. Even Adam made a guest appearance, sitting behind his desk and explaining to her that her employee insurance policy did not cover getting blown up by a bomb. In the background a phone had rung incessantly.

Laura gave up on her hair and straightened the bed. She had donned the old sweatshirt again, even though it had a few holes in it. All the clothes she had brought with her were fit for late summer in Paris, not fall in the Yukon, and the clothes in the closet were of the same caliber as the sweats. Thank goodness for her jeans.

She desperately wanted to call Adam. She wanted an update on the car bomb investigation. None of the radio reports she'd listened to since leaving Montreal had said anything about a bomb. Ditto the online newspapers. Adam would know what was going on.

But Adam's phone could be bugged. The last thing she wanted was to lead Johnny T.'s goons right to her and Fay. They might already know where she was. Who had called last night? There was no way to know.

Fay's ancient phone didn't display incoming phone numbers.

The news magazine was due out today. She would wait until tomorrow to call Adam. She shouldn't have called him from the Toronto diner, but she had wanted to reassure him she was all right. After five years of working for him at the magazine, and running into him for three years before that when she worked for Reuters, he was more a friend than a boss. They had even come close to being more than friends, once.

Three reporters and Adam had been working crazy hours on a vote-splitting scandal out of Ottawa. Adam had set up his command center in his hotel room, managing and editing the stories before they were e-mailed to head office. Laura's was the last story to go and they had ended up alone in his room, celebrating with Glenlivet.

"Good job, Laura," said Adam, toasting her for the third time.

"Couldn't have done it without you," said Laura, enjoying herself tremendously. She was sitting at the window seat, admiring the view of the Rideau Canal at night. She felt lightheaded from the scotch and almost giddy with the relief of meeting the deadline. Adam, standing next to her by the window, evidently felt the same. As she smiled up at him, his expression suddenly changed, as if he were seeing her for the first time. Then he kissed her.

It was a nice kiss, firm and gentle, experienced but not rude. Laura relaxed into it, aware of Adam's warmth and itching to lean into him. A warm tingle began to make its way up her body. Then his hand was on her breast and she came to her senses.

She broke the kiss and moved away from him. "I may be drunk," she told him with a grin, "but I'm not drunk enough to sleep with my boss." And she went back to her own room, alone.

The next morning they greeted each other with sheepish grins and shared painkillers. They never mentioned the incident, but between them was a new intimacy.

Laura sighed. It would be nice to hear Adam's voice again, but she would just have to wait.

Sticking her head out the door, she listened for signs of her mother. Nothing. She must still be in the sewing room.

Laura stepped down into the living room. They couldn't leave the conversation at that. They had never been close, but Fay was still her mother. If she was unhappy, it was Laura's duty to help.

But the study beckoned, and feeling like a coward, she slipped through the study's French doors and immersed herself in the solace of her father's sanctum.

She sank into the brown leather club chair, strategically placed to take advantage of the light streaming through the window. Dad had loved to read here. From this angle, she could see only sky, and part of the cliff, now rusty with fall. From the chair behind the desk, she would be able to view the drop off, and part of the cliff on the other side of the river.

How should she approach Fay? If she had fought with her dad, they would already have made up by now. But she and Fay never argued, never fought, only tiptoed politely around each other. This glimpse into a mother she had never suspected made her uncomfortable. How was she supposed to react?

Laura stood up and went to the bookshelves. There were mostly technical books on accounting principles and case studies, but several bookshelves contained books on history, aerodynamics, engineering and landscaping. Dad hadn't been much on fiction, although a few of his favorites, mostly classics, stood out among the dry subjects like wildflowers in a field of hay. Laura traced a finger along one spine and pulled the book out—*Moby Dick*. Had he actually read it?

"Laura."

Laura dropped the book.

"Sorry." Fay stood behind her, a small smile playing on her lips.

"Tit for tat," grumbled Laura, picking up the book and replacing it on the shelf.

"I've been meaning to clean out those shelves and donate the books." Fay stood hesitantly in the doorway, as if waiting for an invitation.

"Donate them?" A totally irrational resentment rushed through Laura and words burst out of her before she could hold them back. "You can't get rid of Dad's stuff!"

Fay looked as if she'd been slapped. "They're only books, Laura. Do you plan to take up accounting?"

"That's not the point and you know it," said Laura. She had gone too far, but she wasn't about to back down now, especially not when her mother used that tone of voice.

"Exactly what is the point, Laura?" asked Fay, her voice dangerously soft. "That your father was a saint and should now be worshipped? That the wrong parent died?"

"Fay!" Laura swallowed her shock, allowing anger to roll over, submerge, conceal the raw pain behind her mother's words. "What complete bullshit." In two long strides she brushed past her mother.

"This was a mistake," she said grimly. "You and I never could spend time together."

She left through the back door, slamming it in a fit of childishness she knew she would regret.

* * *

Fay remained in the doorway. Across the desk from her, the ghost of her husband wavered before the window, staring sadly at her.

"Get out!" she suddenly screamed. She grabbed the first book she could lay her hands on and hurled it at the apparition. "Get out, get out, get out!"

Not waiting to see if he obeyed, she ran out of the house, ran to the bench by the cliff, the one he had built for her far enough from the edge that she could sit and enjoy the view without fear. She collapsed on it and hid her face in her hands.

What did they all *want* from her?

After a moment, she realized she could hear rain falling. Surprised, she dropped her hands and opened her eyes. The sunny day remained in front of her, sun glinting off the far away ribbon of river. The sound came from behind her.

She twisted to look back at the house just as the door slammed shut, startling her. The house was shrouded in night and rain, but it was not her house. It was the house as it was when they were building it.

Her heart lurched then thudded painfully against her ribs.

James stood on the makeshift porch, squinting into the night. The wind drove raindrops against his face, plastering his hair to his head. It was James as he had been over thirty years ago.

A hundred feet away, a lessening in the darkness betrayed the cliff's edge. Between the wind rushing through the pines and the rain pelting the unfinished side of the house, she could barely hear the river.

James turned up the collar of his denim jacket. She remembered that jacket. She had given it to him. The rain penetrated the heavy fabric within seconds.

He set off down the cliff trail and Fay scrambled to her feet to follow him. The rain pounded down but she remained dry, as did the path beneath her feet. She walked in daylight but her husband hunched his shoulders against the cold and wet.

He was heading for the cabin Sawyer Leduc used to rent from him. That was how she had met Sawyer, running into him one day when they were both on the trail. It veered close to the cliff's edge and James kept his head down, placing his feet carefully on the slippery path. Fay avoided looking at the edge, her stomach doing its familiar flip.

And then Sawyer was there, blocking the way.

"James." Sawyer waited, a tall, lean figure, face invisible in the darkness.

Fay gasped, as much for air as for the shock of hearing Sawyer's beloved voice again. At twenty-four, Sawyer had been closer to her age than James's thirty. A flush of guilt ran through her. They had been friends until she came between them.

Sawyer's shoulders were hunched against the rain, too. "I was coming to see you."

James stopped. "About Fay."

Sawyer came closer. "Yes."

"You know we're getting married."

Sawyer laughed, the sound muted by the drumming of rain on leaves. "Marriage? Don't pressure her, man. Let her decide for herself what she wants to do."

James's voice was hard. "It's what *you* want that doesn't matter anymore, Sawyer. Fay's marrying me. Stop playing games with her."

Fay wiped at the tears on her cheeks. Why were they doing this?

And suddenly she knew which night this was. In spite of the heat of the sun, she felt cold. She wrapped her arms around herself and shivered. It was the night she and Sawyer were supposed to run away together. The night he never came for her.

Oblivious to her presence, Sawyer shifted. "No games, man, and you know it. Fay loves me, not you."

James closed the gap between them in one stride and grabbed the younger man's leather jacket.

"I want you out of that cabin and off my land by tomorrow morning. Is that clear, *man?*"

"I'll go, James, but she's coming with me." Sawyer shoved hard against James's chest.

The wet leather slipped out of James's fingers and Fay clamped a hand over her mouth. Her heart beat wildly.

Surprised by his abrupt freedom, Sawyer lurched back. "Jesus!" He flailed his arms, suddenly aware of the danger.

"Watch out!" cried James. He grabbed for Sawyer, but the other man stepped back again, fighting to regain his balance. His booted heel landed on a rock wet with rain and moss, and it slid from beneath his foot.

"Oh God," whispered Fay.

"Sawyer!" James's hand closed over empty air, and he watched in horror as the dark shape that was Sawyer fell silently off the cliff.

The vision faded as quickly as it had appeared, leaving the sun to shine on Fay's devastation. Sawyer hadn't abandoned her. He had wanted her, had come for her, and James had stopped him.

CHAPTER FIVE

T he sky was achingly blue, so blue it brought tears to Laura's eyes. She followed the cliff trail, walking fast to outdistance the little voice telling her she was an ass.

The river tumbled below and she lost herself in its rhythm. At least *that* hadn't changed while she was gone. After a few minutes, the sound of hammering broke through the river's song and she stopped. She was on Mack's land.

She should go back, apologize to Fay and try to understand this stranger who was her mother.

Instead, she kept going. The hammering got louder, echoing against the far cliff wall. She angled through the trees toward the sound until a clearing revealed the construction site, about forty feet away. The hammering stopped, and she stepped behind a tree to watch. If Mack had company, she wanted to be able to slip away without being seen.

His house was maybe thirty feet by twenty-five. On the wall facing her, at basement level, three large window openings were covered with clear plastic. On the main floor, two bare-bones walls met in a corner, with cross braces providing precarious support. Piles of lumber were stacked next to a table saw at the closest end of the building.

Through the wall studs she saw Mack perched on a sawhorse, drinking something from a steaming thermos. In spite of the chill he was naked from the waist up and his back glistened with sweat. He was alone.

Laura studied the contours of his muscled back, swallowed hard and turned away. She leaned against the big poplar and considered her options. She wasn't dressed warmly enough to spend the day wandering about outside. That left going back home and facing her mother, or joining Mack.

The memory of that naked, glistening back intruded on her thoughts.

"Laura? Is that you?"

Laura stood very still. How had he known she was there?

Taking a deep breath, she stepped away from the tree and turned to face the house. Mack was standing between two wall studs at the edge of the floor, looking straight at her. He had donned a T-shirt.

"Are you all right?" he asked.

Not really, she thought. She felt like a fool. What was she doing lurking in the woods, spying on a strange man? Good grief.

"I'm fine," she said, staring up at him.

"Let me show you around the house," said Mack. "It's not much yet, but it's getting there."

Laura emerged from the woods and walked to where he waited for her. With a smile he indicated the planks bridging the gap to the house. She gingerly crossed the makeshift bridge and followed him through the framed doorway. She tried not to notice how the muscles played beneath his blue T-shirt or how well he filled his jeans. From the two brief glimpses she'd had, she knew his back and chest were smooth. What would it be like to stroke that smooth skin with her hands? Would tiny hairs prickle?

Snap out of it, she told herself grimly. *Think of something else.*

"How did you know I was out here?"

Mack looked back at her, as if debating whether or not to answer. The sun caught glints of gold in his thick brown hair. Finally he turned to face her.

"Your mother called. She was going to town and said you might be coming this way. She asked would I let you know she'd be back by supper. Would I keep an eye on you."

His tone invited explanation, but Laura couldn't speak. She was mortified that her mother would ask Mack to keep watch on her, as if she were a little kid who had run away from home to the neighbor's. Pat, pat.

How the hell did Fay know where she had gone? And what right did she have to involve this man in her affairs?

The right of a mother, apparently.

Laura glanced over her shoulder at the beckoning woods, wishing she had never come back home.

Some of what she was feeling must have shown on her face.

"Hey—Laura…" He took her hand in his, as if to prevent her escape. Warmth engulfed her cold fingers and she looked down at her hand in surprise. The feel of his callused fingers against her skin sent a shiver up her arm. His hand travelled to her shoulder and she looked up into his face, searching.

"Laura…"

For a moment, the anticipation of his kiss vibrated in the air around her. Then he released her and stepped back.

"Don't be mad at your mom," he said. "It's her job to worry." A slow smile spread over his face and she caught her breath. "If you have nothing better to do today," he added, "why don't you stick around and help me build walls? I'll feed you." His tone suggested that food would be ample payment for a day of hard labor.

Laura didn't know whether to be disappointed or relieved he hadn't kissed her.

"Well… if you promise to feed me…" She grinned at him and felt her spirits lift for the first time that day. This was definitely better than an empty house and mysterious phone calls.

First, he led her back down the planks and around the house to where the slope of the land allowed for ground level entry. A heavy metal door opened onto a large basement bisected by a support wall. One half of the room was living quarters, with a long counter down part of one wall. A kitchen sink was set in the middle of the counter. Next to the counter was a gleaming black refrigerator. A microwave and hotplate sat on the counter next to a pile of stacked dishes. The dining room consisted of a round patio table with four plastic white chairs. A thick foam pad topped by a sleeping bag lay on the floor at the far end of the room.

Following her gaze, Mack grinned.

"My real furniture is in storage. No sense risking the good stuff in a construction zone."

In the opposite corner, glimpsed through the studs of the support wall, sat a heavy duty woodstove. Tools and equipment filled the other end of the room.

Hardly luxurious, but it probably beat camping out in a wall tent.

Outside, Mack set Laura to measuring and cutting studs on the table saw while he worked on framing the wall. He kept an eye on her, but she knew enough to keep her fingers away from the blade. After a while she grew warm and removed her sweatshirt. She caught Mack looking at her a few times and grew even warmer.

She found herself hyperaware of his movements, of the way the breeze lifted strands of his hair and how the shadows of the studs played on his back as he hammered nails in.

Pay attention, she told herself firmly, focusing on the table saw. Still, she noticed when he reached into a cooler and brought out two water bottles. She shut off the table saw before accepting one from him.

"You expect to be done before the snow flies?" she asked. Her ears rang from the sudden silence.

He shrugged, drawing her eyes to his muscled shoulders. It took an effort to drag her gaze back up.

"I've got these two outer walls to put up before the roof trusses get here day after tomorrow. Then I can get going on the roof. After that, it'll go fast."

Laura glanced around the clearing. Lots of yellow in the poplars and rust in the fireweed. Mornings were already crusty with frost.

"Well, good luck," she said doubtfully. And then, because she was nosy, she added, "Nice of your boss to give you all this time off."

He smiled. "Subtlety is not your strong suit, Laura." She grinned unrepentantly and he continued. "I have a surveying company in town. I pop in every other day, but mostly my office manager is keeping things going."

He took a last swallow of water and tossed the empty into a plastic bag in the corner before getting back to hammering. Laura took a moment longer to finish her water and then went back to work.

* * *

Before she knew it, it was time for lunch.

They sat on sawhorses, eating meat sandwiches and drinking cold beer, while Mack explained the next step. He had marked on the frame where the studs were to go, at sixteen-inch intervals. Laura would hold the stud in place while he hammered. Once they were all in, they would haul the wall up, hammer in the base and the braces, and start in on the last wall.

"Sounds pretty easy," commented Laura around a mouthful of food. She had already polished off one thick sandwich and was working her way through a second one.

"Remember we have to frame in the windows and doors, too."

This was a far cry from working out in the gym. It reminded her of fall days spent in the bush with her parents, cutting their winter's supply of wood. Hard work, but satisfying.

It took three hours to finish the wall, its doorway and two windows. By the time they stood back to admire it, the sun cast long shadows and the surrounding trees had taken on the dreamy quality of late afternoon in the North. Laura groaned with effort as she and Mack pried crowbars under the wall to lift it. They managed to get their fingers under the heavy wall and hoist it up a few feet.

"Okay," grunted Mack. "I'll hold it up—get a couple of sawhorses to support it."

Laura let go of her end and ran for the sawhorses. She placed one at her end of the wall and the other at Mack's. With a sigh of relief he lowered the wall to the sawhorses, then walked over to pile of tools in the corner, startling a squirrel, which ran off chittering. He rummaged around and returned with a length of nylon rope.

"I'll go down on the ground and haul," he told Laura, tying the rope at the top of the wall. "You push and keep it steady once it's up. Can you do that?"

Laura eyed the wall dubiously. She was strong, but the wall was heavy. "We won't know until we try."

"Now *that's* reassuring," teased Mack. He placed a warm hand on her shoulder. "Just give me enough warning to get out of the way before you drop it on me."

Intensely aware of his hand, Laura could only nod.

With one end of the rope in hand, Mack jumped to the ground.

"Ready?" he called.

"Okay."

The rope grew taut and she lifted the wall off the sawhorses. It was surprisingly easy until the wall was almost perpendicular to the floor.

"Slow down!" called Laura. "It'll flip over onto you!"

Immediately the rope grew slack and she took the weight of the wall on her outstretched arms. She braced her feet and leaned into the weight, wondering if there was any way she could avoid serious injury.

"Got it, Laura?" called Mack. "Hang on, I'll be right there."

And he was. Within seconds, he was at one end of the wall, helping support it. They inched the wall into place with a sledgehammer and he nailed it to the floor, then nailed two cross braces to steady it.

"There," he said, stepping back with satisfaction.

"There," she agreed, standing next to him. It really was a thing of beauty.

"Now then." Mack turned to her. "Are you going to tell me why you're hiding from your husband?"

The question took Laura completely by surprise. She looked at him, confused. "My what?"

"The fellow you had me lie to on the phone last night," he reminded her. "Isn't he your husband?"

Laura blushed. She felt the heat on her cheeks and shook her head. "No. I'm not married."

"Boyfriend?" His blue eyes seemed very dark suddenly.

"No," she whispered, her eyes riveted on his.

"Any romantic attachments at all?" He stepped closer.

She seemed to have lost her voice. All she could do was shake her head.

A fierce light came into his eyes.

"Me neither," he said. Placing both callused hands on her cheeks, he bent toward her mouth. At the last moment, just as she was closing her eyes, he paused and looked at her. Satisfied that she was willing, he kissed her.

He smelled of sweat, and sun, and fresh air, and his mouth was firm and hot. He explored her lips with his, kissing the corners of her mouth and the swell of her bottom lip. Just as she felt she would melt with wanting him, he released her.

"Thank you," he said gravely. "I've been wanting to do that since yesterday."

Laura struggled to regain her mental balance. She cleared her throat. "You're welcome," she finally replied. "Glad I could oblige."

His eyes danced with laughter. He took her hand and led her to a sawhorse. Once she was seated, he cleared the other sawhorse of tools, dragged it close to hers and sat down.

"If it's not a husband you're hiding from, who is it? What was it about that phone call that had you so scared?"

Laura looked at him and sighed. Fay had firmly changed the topic last night, and Mack had gone along. Apparently today he was going to insist. She wanted to confide in him. She was sure she could trust him, but lust might be coloring her judgment.

Still, what harm could there be? The magazine was out today—that was obviously the reason Fay had gone into town. With the story out in the public, it wouldn't matter who knew where Laura was.

And if the story wasn't there?

With regret she decided she couldn't risk it until she knew for sure. It was bad enough she had involved her mother. She didn't have the right to risk his life, too.

"I can't tell you," she said. She wanted to soften the words, to give him some reassurance that her decision wasn't a reflection on him, but she was wise enough to know more words wouldn't help.

He studied her face for a moment and finally nodded, accepting her decision. "You'll eventually be free to tell me?"

She nodded, relieved.

"Fine. I guess I'll wait."

"Mack…" She paused, not quite knowing how to ask. "It's very important that no one know where I am."

His face grew still. "No one?"

"Absolutely no one."

"Is that why you were sneaking around your own house yesterday?"

Laura grinned. "And I would have gotten away with it, too, if you didn't like hot showers."

He blushed and she laughed.

"At least tell me why you and Fay were fighting."

Laura's eyebrows rose. "What makes you think we were fighting?"

Mack shrugged. "She sounded upset. Then you showed up, skulking in the woods as if you were hiding from something. It doesn't take a genius to figure out you had an argument."

Laura shrugged. She stood up and paced to the wall. "We don't get along. Dad and I were very close, and I think she always resented it." She looked at him, suddenly sad. "She never understood me the way he did."

"Oh please," he scoffed. "Next you'll say she doesn't really love you and she's to blame for all your problems. You're supposed to outgrow that crap when you're an adult."

He sat perched on the sawhorse, long legs crossed at the ankles, arms crossed, staring at her. Although he smiled sardonically, something in his eyes had changed. He was disappointed in her.

Who the hell did he think he was?

The sudden bleat of his cell phone saved her from replying angrily. He stood up. "Excuse me," he said, and turned away to take the call.

Laura watched him for a second longer, then stalked to the edge of the floor. She jumped down, landing on the mossy ground with a soft thud. Behind her, Mack interrupted his telephone conversation to call out, "Laura, wait!"

Back stiff, she kept walking. Her eyes filled with tears of rage.

How dare he pass judgment on her relationship with Fay. He didn't know her at all—a kiss didn't entitle him to preach!

The tears streamed down her face, enraging her further. She hadn't wept since her father died, and now this sanctimonious stranger was making her cry!

She found the path by luck more than anything and broke into a run. She would go back to Fay's house and if the article was there, she would take the first plane back to Montreal. She'd had enough of this emotional merry-go-round.

The trail veered briefly away from the cliff and as she entered the shadowy woods, she realized she had forgotten her sweatshirt at Mack's. Well, she wasn't going back. The tears stopped and she slowed to a walk, breathing hard. It was hard to sustain rage when she was gasping for breath.

A shiver ran up her arms and she rubbed them. She slowed down even more, suddenly uneasy in the dark woods. It seemed very quiet.

The setting sun blinded her as she emerged from the trees. She blinked, and then her eye caught a flicker of movement. She turned her head, forgetting to breathe. A young man stood among the shadows. He was tall and wore jeans and a leather jacket. His hands hung by his sides, empty. He was no more than ten feet from her, and she clearly saw his hazel eyes and light brown hair. He frowned at her.

Then he was gone.

Laura blinked again and scanned the trees slowly. There was nowhere for him to disappear to. But there was no trace of him.

She let her breath out slowly. Somebody had been there. She wasn't crazy. So where was he?

A thrill of fear coursed through her, thoroughly displacing her anger. She began running again, stumbling at first until she found her pace. She settled into a ground-eating lope, trying to watch the path and the woods at the same time. Maybe he was another neighbor… He hadn't had a gun that she could see. Maybe she was overreacting, but she didn't stop running until Fay's house was in sight.

She slowed to a walk, gasping and holding her side, trying to breathe through a stitch. She glanced over her shoulder at the trail, but nobody followed. The garage door was open, and Fay's car was there. Relief washed through her.

The front door opened and Fay stepped into the dying light. Her face was pale as she stared at her daughter.

"Fay?" said Laura, suddenly afraid. She looked down and saw that Fay was clutching a magazine.

"It's not there, Laura." Fay took a deep breath. "Your article isn't there."

CHAPTER SIX

Fay came down a step and stopped. She wanted to reach out to her daughter, but the weight of the words they had thrown at each other that morning pinned her down. She wasn't at all sure Laura would welcome comforting from her.

A sudden noise made her glance up just as Laura spun around. Someone was pounding up the path. Laura looked about frantically and finally dove into the open garage. Fay stared after her, expecting the car to roar to life, but Laura returned with an axe just as Mack emerged from the trees. Fay looked from Laura to Mack, baffled.

Mack eyed the axe warily but was too winded to speak. He bent over, hands on knees, and concentrated on catching his breath.

Fay stared the question at Laura.

"There was a man in the woods," said Laura. "Not Mack. Someone else." She let the axe head drop to the ground and leaned on the handle, as if she no longer trusted her legs.

Fay scanned the trees surrounding them, acutely aware of their vulnerability. The wind riffled the treetops and swirled leaves around the gravel driveway.

"I didn't see anyone," said Mack, finally straightening.

Laura eyed him coldly. "Well, I did."

"Let's go inside," said Fay. She didn't know what had sent both her daughter and Mack running up the path, but if someone was out there, she wanted to be inside. All this anxiety over an article… She hoped John Tucker would spend a long time behind bars.

Fay stepped back and allowed them to precede her, then locked the door. They trooped up to the kitchen and Mack immediately went to stand by the window, staring out. Laura took the magazine from Fay and sat down at the table to look through it. She kept her back to Mack.

It's distinctly chilly in here, thought Fay.

"What did he look like?" she asked her daughter. As she spoke, her question conjured up a tingling suspicion. Then Laura described him, and Fay closed her eyes. Sawyer.

Relief robbed her legs of strength and she sat down heavily. "He's no danger to you," she managed to say. Dear God, Laura had seen Sawyer.

She wasn't crazy after all.

"You know who it is?" asked Mack, turning from the window. Concern and curiosity radiated from him. "How long has he been hanging around? Why didn't you tell me about him? Does he live around here?"

Fay realized he had a right to know if strangers were hanging around, but she couldn't think of anything to tell him that wouldn't sound crazy, so she smiled at him and shrugged.

If she tried to explain, she knew she would start crying. Sawyer had come for her, and James had stopped him. The Yukon River had swallowed him up and never released him.

His death had been an accident and clearly both men had wanted her to know that. But all those years she had wondered…

60

Had James truly been that angry at her?

Mack looked from Fay's smile to Laura's frown with frustration.

"Will someone please tell me what's going on?"

"Yes, Fay," agreed Laura. "What's going on?"

Fay couldn't tell them. How could she? They would think loneliness had unhinged her. Maybe it had. But it was *her* madness, *her* past, and she chose not to share.

Yet Laura had seen Sawyer. Was this *folie à deux?* Was the haunting going to extend to her daughter now? She had to put an end to this.

"He's no danger," she repeated. Laura looked as if she would pursue the matter, but Fay cut her off. "Why were you running, Mack?"

Mack looked uncomfortable. His color was still high from the run, and now it deepened. "I wanted to talk to Laura."

Fay glanced at her daughter, who resolutely refused to look at Mack. So. They'd already managed to quarrel. Was that a good sign or a bad one?

"What are you going to do now?" she asked her daughter.

A curious mix of emotions flitted across Laura's face— determination, desperation, anger. But all she said was, "Can I borrow your car?"

Fay hesitated. "To do what?" Was she going to run again?

"I need to call Adam," said Laura, "and I don't want to call from here. I'll find a pay phone downtown."

"Who the hell is Adam?" asked Mack, frustration making his voice sharp.

"My boss," said Laura. She turned back to Fay. "I want you to get out of here. Go to Sally's, stay there for the night. Just in case."

"Sally's?" Fay repeated. Go to her friend's house and maybe drag along whatever troubles were following them? "No," she said firmly. "I'm going with you."

Laura took a deep breath. "Fay…" As if at a loss for words, she stood up and began pacing. The gloom in the kitchen was becoming more pronounced and Fay stood up to turn on the overhead fixture, flooding the room with cheerful light. Mack stepped away from the window to watch Laura.

Laura looked very young in the light, and Fay remembered that particular expression from when her daughter was a child, and trying to persuade her. Earnest. Laura looked very earnest.

"Fay," began Laura again, stopping in front of her mother. To Fay's shock Laura reached out and took her hands. Laura stared at her mother's hands for a long moment, then looked up.

"Mom. Please. Please trust me when I ask you to do this. You say that man in the woods isn't someone to worry about, but I *am* worried. You don't know these people. I wonder now if the phone calls haven't been from Adam trying to warn me, although I don't know how he could have found me. Please believe that I have cause to worry. I…I don't think I could stand it if something happened to you."

Fay's throat tightened as the hurtful words she had thrown at her daughter came back to her. How could she have been so cruel?

She couldn't remember the last time Laura had called her Mom. At that moment she would have done anything her daughter asked. Except abandon her. She had worried about Laura when she was in Kiev, about the political instability and the chronic food shortages. Even the care packages she sent were constantly intercepted. But at least Laura hadn't been in physical danger. Now that she was back home, where she was supposed to be safe, Laura chose to write about biker gangs and smuggling.

Fay shook her head. She freed a hand and cupped her daughter's cheek with it.

"Laura, I couldn't stand it if something happened to you either."

Laura looked confused. She let go of Fay's hand and moved to the window, staring past her reflection into the deepening gloom.

"I can move faster by myself, Fay," she said to the glass. "If worse comes to worst, I can run. Could you keep up?"

The logic of Laura's statement hung in the kitchen like a pall. No, she couldn't keep up. She was in good shape, but she wasn't a runner. If worse came to worst, she would be a liability to her daughter.

"I'll drive Laura into town," said Mack, startling both women. He faced Laura, arms crossed. "Nobody will associate you with my truck. Fay can stay at my place."

But Laura was already shaking her head.

"The danger is just as real for you," she said sharply. "If they see you with me, you could be hurt."

"I'm willing to take that chance."

"I'm not," retorted Laura. "I go alone."

"Then you'll have to walk," said Fay, smiling gently to take the sting out.

"Fay!" Laura frowned at her mother. "Would you really make me walk?"

No, thought Fay. *But this is one fight you're not going to win, my darling daughter.*

"Is she always so contrary?" asked Mack, addressing the comment to Fay.

"Worse," warned Fay. "She's toning it down because of you."

Laura's mouth tightened. Then she caught her mother's smile and a sheepish grin slowly erased her frown.

"Look," she said, glancing from Fay to Mack, then back to Fay. "I know you're both worried. So am I. I need to get to town, but I won't risk either of you. Fay, spend the night at Mack's. You'll be safe there. And Mack, please look out for my mother."

To Fay's surprise she found herself fighting back tears. Laura was concerned about her. In her own prickly way, Laura was trying to protect her.

"So it's agreed." Mack looked at Fay. "You'll stay at my place tonight. I'll drive Laura to town. She can make her phone call and we'll be back before you're ready for bed. Deal?"

"Deal!" agreed Fay, immensely relieved.

"Wait a minute," said Laura. "I made it clear…"

"Don't bother arguing," said Fay. "You're outvoted."

* * *

They left Fay in the basement of Mack's unfinished house. He even had a television set, which Laura hadn't noticed earlier.

Mack made a fire in the woodstove and placed a chair and a light close by for Fay. Then he laid a loaded shotgun on the floor by the chair. Fay stared at it a long time before finally nodding. She had brought along a partly completed hand-quilted pillowcase and was already concentrating on it when Laura and Mack drove off.

They bumped down the driveway in the darkness toward Wild Rose Lane. Something in the back of the pickup clanged noisily every time they hit a pothole. The floor of the big Ford was littered with hoses, clamps and so many tools that Laura finally decided to rest her feet on top of the mess rather than try to clear a space.

She glanced at the man sitting next to her. She wished she could see his face.

She was grateful that he hadn't told Fay about their fight. Two fights in the same day, she thought glumly. And what did those fights have in common? Her. Why had she been so brutal to Fay? And why run when she should have stayed behind and tried to fix things?

A wave of shame swamped her and she closed her eyes, remembering Fay's harsh words. *What is the point, Laura? That the wrong parent died?* Was that what Fay thought? Was that what she had allowed her mother to think for three months?

Mack was right. She was too old to keep punishing her mother for the failures of the past. Fay had done her best, and if she hadn't loved her daughter as much as Laura felt she should, well, it wasn't too late to try again. Was it?

The ride smoothed out as they turned onto Wild Rose Lane and Laura opened her eyes. It was too dark to distinguish anything more than the silhouettes of fir trees against the lighter sky. The moon wouldn't be up for another few hours. A rumble in her stomach reminded her she hadn't eaten supper yet. The dashboard clock read just shy of seven o'clock.

"You're a good runner." Mack's voice came out of the dark.

Is he reaching out, she wondered, *or just trying to be polite?*

"I usually run every day," she replied, then winced. *Don't be such a coward,* she berated herself. *Apologize to the man and get it over with!*

"Laura, I shouldn't have said what I did," said Mack. "I was way out of line and I apologize."

Oh great, now he beat you to it.

"You have nothing to apologize for," she said. Her tone was stilted, even to her ears, so she continued. "You were right, and I was asking for it."

"Hm."

"Hm?"

He turned to look at her, a shadowy movement.

"Exactly what were you asking for?"

Heat rose to Laura's cheeks and she was suddenly glad for the dark. They reached the highway and turned toward town.

"I should tell you a few things, since you insist on coming along."

"About time," he grumbled.

She sighed. "I wish you had stayed behind."

Stop it, stop it, stop it, she told herself. *At least be honest with yourself, if you can't be honest with others. You could have insisted or waited until he was gone and taken Fay's car. You didn't because you wanted him with you.*

"Actually," she said, before he could speak, "that's not true. I'm glad you came."

A quick turn of his head in the dark indicated surprise. "Really? I thought I forced myself on you."

"You did," she pointed out. "But I'm glad of your company. Although you may change your mind when you find out what's going on."

"Which is…?"

So she gave him the bare bones. She told him about Johnny Tucker and his growing network of informants and thugs. She told him about the drug smuggling on two coasts and the car bomb, and hitchhiking to Whitehorse, and the phone calls. She told him about the magazine and how her article wasn't in it.

He listened in silence until she was through, and then kept silent for a few minutes more. She let him digest the information.

There was more traffic coming from town than going—the last stragglers, working late. Every set of headlights blinded her as she herself chewed over a few puzzles.

What was going on in her mother's life that a strange man in the woods was no cause for worry? Where had he disappeared to? What was Fay keeping secret?

Tonight, she decided. As soon as all this was settled, she would sit down with her mother and ask her.

She looked away from the road, staring at the sky and waiting for the first stars to appear.

Finally Mack stirred. "How is phoning your boss going to help anything?"

"It isn't," said Laura. She took a deep breath. "I'm not going to phone Adam. Something went wrong, obviously, or the article would be in the magazine. Phoning him won't change that, and it might help Johnny T. pinpoint where I am. I'm willing to bet he's got Adam's phone tapped."

"Then why are we going to town?"

She hesitated. Did she really want to tell him everything? He seemed trustworthy, but what if he wasn't? Johnny Tucker was a powerful man. She thought about how she and Mack had met, and how long Fay had known him. He couldn't be involved with Johnny T. The coincidence would be incredible. And she needed him to get where she was going.

"To see Seth Howell."

"Howell. The editor of the *Daily Trib?*"

She nodded, then remembered he couldn't see. "Yes. I worked summers for him while I was at college and his son is a friend of mine. They're both newspaper men. I'm hoping Mr. Howell will put the story on the wire."

"Why not find a computer and send it out yourself? I know Fay doesn't have one but we could stop by my office…"

Laura was already shaking her head. "A good option, and thank you. Seth will have all the addresses to the news desks. One quick e-mail and it'll go out to everybody."

She could just make out his nod in the dark.

"You've got it with you?"

"It's easy to access," she hedged. Why didn't she tell him the flash drive was in her pocket? It hadn't been out of her reach since she left Montreal. Maybe she had grown paranoid. "Friday's a heavy paper day. He'll still be in the office, since he always works late on Wednesdays and Thursdays."

"To the *Trib* it is," said Mack, and he fell into an easy silence.

Laura also didn't tell him about sending copies of the article to three different people. Those copies were supposed to arrive by courier tomorrow. Adam would miss out on the scoop. That was too bad, but she wasn't waiting around anymore. She wanted out of this quagmire.

Her name still needed to be on the article, or she would have no protection from Johnny Tucker's revenge. She doubted the Crown Attorney's office would publicize her name for her. Even the RCMP would have other things on its mind. And the reporter in Vancouver would probably be miffed she had inadvertently fed Laura the scoop of the decade. She certainly wouldn't announce it.

And if Seth refused to help or wasn't there?

Well, there was always Mack's office.

Satisfied that she was doing everything she could, she forced herself to relax and watched the stars appear in the night sky. The man sitting next to her smelled of fresh air and wood smoke and she spent long minutes considering the aphrodisiac qualities of both. Finally she shook herself. Time to think of something else.

"Is Mack short for anything?" she asked.

The quality of the darkness changed subtly, and her reporter's instincts instantly sat up.

"No."

Hm. "You mean you were named Mack at birth?"

She could now identify the elusive quality that permeated the air. Panic. She was definitely close to something.

It took him a long time to answer.

"No."

Laura turned in the seat to face him. Even though it was too dark to make out his exact expression, enough light emanated from the dashboard to reveal the bunched muscles at his jawline.

Laura smelled blood and closed in for the kill.

"What's your birth name, Mack?

He remained very quiet, and she started to grin.

"Come on, Mack. You know *my* middle name."

He nodded. "May."

She winced but went on ruthlessly. "And your name is…?"

He mumbled something that got lost in the roar of the engine as he accelerated.

"What was that? I missed it." She leaned in.

"Emmett," he said in a low voice. "My mother named me Emmett."

"Emmett." Her grin got wider. "Your mother named you Emmett."

"Yes, Emmett!" he finally burst out. "My name is Emmett. Are you satisfied?"

"Yes, Emmett, I am," she said politely.

There was a pause.

"May?"

"Yes, Emmett?"

"Call me Mack."

"Yes, Mack."

* * *

Ten minutes later Mack said, "We need to stop for gas. There's a service station coming up."

Laura sat up straighter. "Not a good idea."

Mack turned toward her, his face a study in dark hollows and gleaming eyes in the dashboard lights.

"If I'd realized we were going on a clandestine mission tonight, I would have filled up earlier."

Laura could see the gas station up ahead, a small island of light in a sea of darkness. She glanced at the gas gauge. It hovered on empty. With a sigh that admitted defeat, she turned to face the windshield again.

"You would have made a lousy boy scout," she said grumpily.

She thought she heard him snort, but then he pulled in at the highway service station and parked next to the far island.

"Just stay in the truck," he said, turning off the engine and getting out. A number of cars and pickups were parked next to the dark garage, awaiting the mechanic's attention in the morning. The only other vehicle at the gas station was a late-model, bottle green Lexus parked at the pump nearest the entrance.

She heard Mack unscrew the gas cap and insert the nozzle. Gas sloshed out, and she held her breath against the fumes.

An occasional car sped by on the highway, but none turned in. It was past the after-work rush.

Laura relaxed. It would be all right. She turned the ignition key to the battery and watched the gas gauge needle creep up toward full. Soon they'd be on their way again.

Metal rasped against metal as Mack removed the nozzle. He screwed the cap back on and snugged the nozzle into its slot in the pump. With a quick wink at her he jogged over to the convenience store and disappeared inside.

Laura followed his progress. He didn't go straight to the cash register. Instead, he walked up and down aisles, filling his arms with food.

Bless him, thought Laura. *I hope he brings something to drink, too.*

The counter clerk ignored Mack completely, concentrating instead on his paperback. Even from that distance, Laura could see the eruption of pimples on his cheeks.

Then she saw the driver of the Lexus. He stood with his back to her, just beyond the counter, talking on a pay phone. He wore a black leather windbreaker and black jeans. His hair was so blond it looked almost white, and it was tied back in a ponytail.

Laura frowned, staring at his broad back. There was something familiar about that ponytail, but she couldn't place it. Then he turned to watch Mack and she got a look at his profile.

"Jesus H.," she whispered, and ducked down below the window.

Barney Hicklin, one of Johnny Tucker's enforcers. She had seen him in Johnny's company many times, most often at the Paradiso, the Montreal diner Johnny favored. Hicklin was handsome, and vain about his looks. She would recognize that chiseled profile anywhere.

They had found her.

She risked a peek. Hicklin had his back turned again.

Her first reaction was to scream at Mack to get out of there. Then she realized he was in no danger. Hicklin and Johnny T. didn't know about Mack. As long as they didn't realize he was with her, he would be safe.

Any minute now Hicklin would finish his conversation and come out to the car. What if he saw her? What if he knew where Fay lived and was heading out there? What if, not finding her there, he went looking around?

Dread was a lead ball in the pit of her stomach. She swallowed bile. Something hard poked her knee, and the pain galvanized her into action. She searched through the tools and instruments on the floor of the pickup, looking for something sharp. Although the service station was well lit, the pickup's dashboard cast a shadow on the floor. That and her crouched body obscured the view. In desperation she began pulling the tools out from under her and onto the seat. Finally she found a Phillips screwdriver. It would do.

She shoved the tools back onto the floor, at the last minute grabbing a hammer. Then she inched her way up and looked out the window again. Hicklin was off the phone. He was talking to Mack. His back was to her.

"Now or never, kiddo," she told herself, and reached over to open Mack's door. If Hicklin looked over and saw the door open, he would assume Mack hadn't closed it. If he saw the passenger door open, he would look around for said passenger.

She slid out of the driver side door, keeping as low as she could. Before leaving the cover of the truck, she checked again. Mack was still talking to Hicklin. What could they be talking about? The clerk still had his nose in his pocketbook.

Before she could make a run for the Lexus, reason intruded. If Hicklin found his tires suddenly flat, he would be suspicious. She didn't want Barney Hicklin suspicious.

With a groan, she leaned her head against the cold metal of the truck. She had to get back inside and hide. It was her only chance.

Another peek revealed both men making their way to the cash register. Mack was gesticulating at Hicklin and Laura finally understood that Mack was giving him directions.

She hoped he had the sense to point him the wrong way.

She slithered back into the pickup and sneaked a look. Hicklin was counting his change. Mack was staring straight at her, his expression blank, as if he was waiting for his turn to pay. But his one free hand, out of sight of Hicklin, was gesturing madly at her, waving her away. He wanted her to leave.

Her heart sinking, Laura turned the key in the ignition. The engine roared to life and she glanced nervously at the station. Hicklin was still busy with the clerk, who seemed to be having trouble getting the change right. Mack caught her eye and nodded slowly, once. Without giving doubt a chance to settle in, she put the truck in gear and pulled out of the service station as quietly as she could.

Heart thudding madly, she turned onto the highway and glanced in the rearview mirror. Hicklin was just coming out of the service station.

He slipped into his car without giving her a glance.

Then the road curved and she lost sight of him.

"Shit," she said softly. She didn't know which way Hicklin turned when leaving the station. He might be speeding away from her, or he might be right on her tail.

She stepped on the gas, hoping Mack knew what he was doing.

CHAPTER SEVEN

Laura parked next to an open red dumpster and killed the lights. The alley was dark and she hesitated a few seconds before turning the engine off, too. In the sudden silence, she leaned her head against the cold steering wheel and listened to the blood pounding in her ears.

She hadn't been followed.

In fact, she hadn't encountered another vehicle from the moment she drove into Whitehorse's tiny business district. If anyone was working in any of the buildings neighboring the newspaper office, they were doing it in the dark. Only a few blocks away, people would be lingering over coffee in a restaurant, or getting ready for the late show at the cinema, or enjoying a drink at the bar before heading home.

But at eight o'clock on a Thursday night, the alley behind the newspaper office was deserted and creepy. She would have preferred to use the front door on Tutshi Street, but besides being locked, it was too exposed, especially with Johnny Tucker so close.

She had been too lax, too stupid… She should never have come back home. If she'd kept moving, he wouldn't have found her so easily.

75

Now Barney Hicklin was in town. Or at least around town. Who else might be out there, hunting her? Any stranger on the street might be after her.

And what about Mack? How did he happen to stop for gas at exactly the spot Hicklin was making a phone call? What if she was a complete and utter fool and Mack had only pretended to give Hicklin directions?

What if Hicklin was heading for Fay?

Her mouth went dry and her empty stomach cramped at the thought. Mack had helped her escape from Hicklin. He wasn't the enemy. He couldn't be.

Could he?

She fought down an impulse to switch on the engine and race back to Fay. She was being paranoid. Mack was doing his level best to help her. Now she had to help herself. The only sure way to protect her mother—and herself—was to get the story out.

Finally she straightened and looked in the rearview mirror. The windows were already fogged with her breath. She rolled down her window part way to let the humidity escape and wiped at the back window with the sleeve of her sweatshirt. Nobody in sight.

She opened the truck door and slid out on unsteady legs. The alley smelled one day shy of garbage pickup. The upper window of the *Daily Tribune* was lit, casting enough light on the alley below to reveal the back door. That window was in Seth Howell's office. She picked her way around potholes and broken glass and tried the doorknob. Locked.

After a brief search she found a few pebbles and an empty Coors Light can. She considered the weight of each and finally dropped the pebbles into the beer can. Taking a deep breath, she swung back and let fly. The can sailed through the air and landed in a rattling slide against the brick next to the window. It fell back to the pavement.

Her second attempt was better. The can connected with the window with a resounding thunk and a clatter of pebbles. It bounced back from the window and landed in the dumpster.

She stared at the smelly container and decided against going in after the can.

With a sigh of frustration, she squinted in the dim light, looking for something else she could use to attract Mr. Howell's attention.

Then the window slid open and she heard a man's voice. "Who's out there?"

Laura looked up and saw, silhouetted against the bright light, a head sticking out of the window.

"Mr. Howell?" she asked, unable to see his face.

"Yeah, and who the hell are you?" said the voice from above.

Laura blinked against the glare. Something about the hair wasn't right.

"Are you Seth Howell?" she demanded, responding to the abruptness in the man's voice.

Silence followed her question, and they stared at each other, Laura in the alley and the man in the window. She edged away from the pool of light. Something was wrong. That wasn't Mr. Howell.

"Is that you, Laura?"

Laura stopped moving, trying to keep the fear inside her from mushrooming.

"I'll be right down," said the man, and suddenly the window was empty again.

Laura headed for the truck. Maybe he was a friend, but she wasn't taking a chance. She climbed in and turned the engine on just as the back door to the newspaper opened. Bright light spilled through, blinding her, and a tall figure stepped into the alley. He headed for her and Laura put the truck in reverse but kept her foot on the brake. Just in case.

"Laura?" The man stepped up to the driver's door and for the first time, she got a good look at him.

"Jason? I didn't recognize your voice."

"Jesus, Laura, it is you! Why didn't you say so?"

Jason Howell waited while she turned the engine off and got out of the truck, then he swept her into a bear hug that left her breathless.

"Is it ever good to see you!" He beamed at her.

She smiled back weakly. "It's good to see you, too," she said. And it was. They had known each other throughout high school but only started hanging out together when she worked summers at the paper. Jason had been away at college, too, and came back to work for his dad during the summer. He followed his father into the newspaper business, just as his father had followed his.

They'd had fun together. When college ended, he went to work in Vancouver for a big daily. Jason and his dad loved each other but knew better than to try working together on a long-term basis.

"This is silly," said Jason. He took her hand and pulled her toward the door. "Why are we standing in a dark alley when we could be sitting in my dingy office? Come on."

Laura allowed him to lead her inside. She needed a few minutes to think through what to do. She had counted on Seth Howell being there.

A bare bulb in the stairwell lit the cement steps. "Where's your dad?" asked Laura as they reached the top floor, where the newspaper office was. The adrenaline was slowly subsiding, leaving her feeling shaky. Or maybe that was hunger.

"Geez, Laura, didn't you know?" He turned to look at her, his wonderful, plain face somber. "Dad had a stroke about a month ago. I'm running the paper now."

"Oh, Jason," whispered Laura. She pressed a palm against his chest. "I'm so sorry."

Jason placed his big hand over hers, warming her. "He's at home, recuperating," he said. "He's actually not that bad, but I guess he decided it was time to take it easy. He's sixty-eight, you know. He'd love to see you."

Laura closed her eyes. "This isn't a very good time. Please give him my love."

Jason looked at her curiously, but he didn't say anything. He led the way through the darkened layout area to Seth's office, where a fluorescent light exposed carpets that had been decrepit a decade ago.

"When are you going to change the carpets, Jason?" she couldn't resist asking.

He grinned at her, recognizing their old joke.

"The workers are coming next week to rip out the old carpet and lay some tile instead. Too many people were complaining about allergies."

Laura nodded. Mr. Howell hadn't been too keen on making changes, especially expensive ones.

As they entered Jason's office, she caught a whiff of emulsifier from the darkroom next door. *Some things never change,* she thought. Most newspapers had gone all digital.

"Have a seat," said Jason, pointing at the old-fashioned swivel chair. She sat down on the carved wooden seat, careful not to lean too far back. She remembered this chair, too.

The office was small and crowded with an oversized desk that must have been placed in the room before the walls were built. Two computers sat on the desk, although only one was on. A line of green ants marched across the screen—a screensaver program. Beneath the only window in the room was a long narrow table. Two four-drawer metal filing cabinets had been shoehorned in on either side of the table. In the days when Mr. Howell ran the paper, every flat surface had been covered in piles of photographs, old newspapers, letters and coffee cups.

Although it still looked like a working office, there were now more surfaces showing, and the piles were neat.

Jason pulled up a stool and sat down in front of her. "Now, why were you trying to break my window?"

She looked at him for a long moment, debating. His clear blue eyes stared back at her, smiling.

She had trusted his judgment as a reporter and as a friend, but was it fair to drag him into her problems like this? He could get hurt.

But how many more people would get hurt if she didn't get the story out?

She'd been prepared to drag his father into it…

He stared back at her, a man in his prime, with just enough lines on his face to make him interesting. Laura couldn't help comparing his brush cut with Mack's shaggy hair. She closed her eyes, hoping Mack was all right.

"Well?

She opened her eyes. "I need your help."

As she began her story, he sat up straighter, but by the time she finished, his forearms rested on his knees, his shoulders were hunched over and his head hung down as he stared at the floor. Laura almost smiled at his classic vulture listening pose.

When she finally stopped talking, he looked up at her.

"Do you have the article with you?"

Laura nodded.

"Let's see it."

She fished in her jeans pocket, fumbled the flash drive out and handed it to him. He held it gingerly, as if it were hot. Then he frowned.

"There was a man here a couple of days ago, asking about you."

Laura clasped her trembling hands tightly in her lap.

"Who was it?"

Jason rubbed his face tiredly then ran his fingers through his brush cut.

"Can't remember his name. He was a tall fellow, with dark eyes and short dark hair, starting to bald a bit in back. He was slim, and according to my office manager, he was definitely hunk material." His attempt at a smile faded when he took in her expression.

The description didn't fit Hicklin, so that answered one question—Johnny Tucker had sent more than one thug after her. She raked her memory, trying to fit the description to a face, but came up blank.

"What did he ask about me?"

"He said he was here on a whitewater rafting trip and used to work with a girl who had worked at the *Trib* and did I remember you. I said yes, you used to work here summers but had left quite a while ago. His questions were a little too intense to be innocent. He fished around for names of family, but I pretended I was too thick to understand. Finally he came right out and asked if you still had family around here. I said I didn't know." He shrugged. "I didn't like him. I escorted him out of the building so he wouldn't ask anyone else." He looked at her. "But there aren't many Thorsens in the phone book. It'd be easy enough to find out where your mother lives."

"Damn!" Laura stood up, longing to pace, but the office was too cramped. "Damn, damn, damn—I have to go, Jason."

He grabbed her by the sweatshirt and forced her to sit down. "Relax. If he really is a bad guy and not some ex-boyfriend lusting after you—" he wiggled his eyebrows suggestively "—then he's had a couple of days. If he was going to do something, he would have done it already. Go get yourself a pop while I read the article."

He swiveled on his stool and slid the drive into a USB port. He hit a key and the marching ants made way for a list of available programs. Laura hesitated a few moments, then decided her original reasoning was still sound. The only way to ensure Fay's safety was to get the story out as soon as possible.

She went to the darkroom, where the refrigerator was kept. The chemical smell grew stronger the closer she came. The curtains were swept away from the door, and she had just enough light to make her way cautiously toward the two refrigerators. The one on the left contained a familiar array of chemicals sealed in plastic bottles, but the right hand one held pop cans in the door. Mustard and ketchup bottles and a selection of small plastic salad dressing containers graced the middle shelf. A container of cream on the top shelf had gone bad, by the smell of it. She looked in the crisper and found gray plastic containers of film. No leftover lunches anywhere.

While the door was open and the light on, she looked around the darkroom. Strings criss-crossed the air between the two farthest walls. A dozen clips hung on the strings, waiting to hold prints up for drying. A long narrow tub at the far end was filled with shallow trays. A table under a red lightbulb completed the furnishings. On the walls were pictures of young, semi-clad women.

Ah, she thought. The paper still had a male photographer.

What about the door? Was it still there? She and some of the younger reporters, including Jason, had used the hidden door to steal a smoke or get away from the office manager, a crab-faced woman who frowned every time someone laughed.

She felt the wall next to the fridge where a ceiling-to-floor heavy black curtain covered the wall. At the edge of the curtain she found the doorknob. In spite of everything, she grinned. She slid back the bolt and cracked the door open. It opened onto empty air. The building next door was less than two feet away, and lower by a foot or so. That roof was ideal for getting fresh air or having a private conversation. She was willing to bet the young reporters still used it.

With a sigh Laura closed and bolted the door. She picked a

ginger ale and returned to Jason's office to find him still engrossed. He looked up as she sat down.

"By the way, I'd been meaning to get in touch with you. I found something when I was cleaning out Dad's files a few weeks ago. It's for you." He pushed away from the computer, reached out a long arm and pulled open the third drawer of the nearest filing cabinet. He plucked an envelope from the front and handed it to her. "I guess your father left this in trust with Dad, to give to you in person."

Laura's stomach did a slow loop. Her father had left something for her? Here?

She stared at the brown manila envelope for a moment before accepting it with trembling fingers. The envelope was open. On the front, in her father's untidy scrawl, was written "Seth".

"Why would he leave it with your father?" she asked. Her fingers caressed the edges of the envelope. "Why not with my mother?"

Jason shrugged. "Dad didn't know. Your father left it with mine almost ten years ago, with instructions to give it to you if he died. I think they both forgot about it. I know my dad did, until I found it." He turned back to his computer screen, probably as much to give her privacy as to finish her story.

Laura finally upended the envelope, only to find another, smaller manila envelope inside. This one had a note clipped to it that read, *Seth—I'm using you as a safety deposit box. If I die before you, please give this to Laura. Wait until the worst of the grieving is over. Thanks, old friend.* Her father had signed it.

This envelope was sealed. Laura looked around and found a letter opener sticking out of a coffee cup on top of the filing cabinet. She slit the envelope open and pulled out the contents.

Two photographs. She peered inside to see if there was a note, but there was nothing else. Puzzled, she looked at the photos. The first one was an old black and white print of a young woman, perhaps twenty-five years old. She wore a long skirt of some light-colored fabric, with a short jacket over a white, frilly blouse. The jacket was decorated with dark braiding. Her dark hair was swept up in a chignon, and perched on one side of her head was a small hat. The woman looked familiar. Laura flipped the photograph over and read, in a clear, neat print: Aunt Gertrude Thorsen, before leaving for the continent—1903.

Another hand, her father's, had written below it, Grandfather's sister.

Laura studied the photograph. It finally registered that Aunt Gertrude looked familiar because she looked like Laura—or Laura looked like her. It was almost like looking in a mirror, even down to the faint scowl on the woman's face. Laura immediately stopped frowning.

If she was Dad's great aunt, that would make her Laura's great-great aunt. Why would her father leave her this picture in such a roundabout way?

She looked at the other one. It was an old snapshot, in glossy color, and the date stamped in small numbers in the bottom of the photo said 1976. Three people sat on the front porch of a cabin, in bright sunlight.

With a shock, Laura recognized her mother. She was smiling at the photographer. Her hair was straight, long and blond, held back by a colorful sweatband across her forehead. She wore a tie-dyed loose shirt and patched jeans. She was gorgeous and looked happy. Sitting beside her on the stairs was Laura's father. He had his arm around Fay and was wearing jeans and sandals, and a psychedelic T-shirt. His hair was down to his collar, a fine, pale brown that looked better shorter. He, too, was looking at the photographer, but his whole body seemed to curve toward Fay—protecting her or guarding her?

The other man sat one step up from them. His elbows rested on his knees, his hands relaxed between them. They were big hands. He, too, wore jeans, but on his feet were solid work boots. He wore a denim shirt open at the collar, and by the looks of it, it had seen better days. Around his neck was a leather thong and a pendant. His hair was light and curly. He was looking at Fay, his pleasant, open face grave.

Laura stared at the man's face for a long, long time. It was the man she had seen in the woods near her mother's house.

Unsettled, she flipped over the snapshot. On the back, someone had written in bold pen: Fay, James and Sawyer—August 1976.

"Jesus," said Jason, sitting back. He turned around, a gleam in his eye. "This is a hell of a story, Laura. Do you have proof?"

Laura slipped the two photographs into their envelope. "Pictures, names and addresses, times and locations on a separate file on the same flash drive. It's all there, Jason."

"No wonder Tucker's after you. What a scoop!"

I used to feel that way too, thought Laura.

"You realize you'll probably get fired for coming to me with it."

She cocked her head at him. "Right now that's the least of my worries."

He grinned. "Good point. It'll be on tomorrow's front page, but I don't think we should wait that long. Can we send it to the news service now?"

"Yes, please." Could it really be this simple?

"All right. But there's no guarantee the news service will pick it up."

Laura raised an eyebrow at him. There was never any guarantee, but she wasn't worried. It was the story of the decade. The service would pick it up. Then the cold spotlight of publicity would be on Johnny Tucker and she and Fay would be safe.

"In fact," added Jason, "I think I'll stack the deck in our favor and send it directly to a few other editors I know."

Turning back to the computer, he called up his e-mail program and began feeding it addresses. He drafted a quick paragraph giving the gist of the story and attached Laura's file to the message.

Laura sat and watched his quick fingers, too emotionally exhausted to register anything but relief. Jason hit the send button and grinned up at her.

Then the screen winked out. A split second later the building plunged into darkness.

Laura's eyes adjusted within seconds. She made out Jason's figure against the incidental light from the window.

"Coincidence?" he asked in a low voice.

"Not likely," she whispered back. "Did the article get out?"

"I don't know," he replied. His figure craned toward the window. "Looks like the rest of the street has electricity. That means someone got to the fuse box in the press room. I vote we get out of here."

"Right behind you, Jase."

She heard the sound of the flash drive being released from the computer and grabbed the envelope with the pictures. Then he was by her side and dragging her through the layout area back to the darkroom. He flicked the curtains closed behind them, cutting off any possible source of light.

Laura's shoulder collided with the refrigerator and Jason lost his grip on her hand. She stepped forward just as he turned around and they bumped into each other.

A sound penetrated the muffling barrier of the darkroom curtains and they grew still, waiting for it to repeat. After a few seconds she heard the swish of the wall curtain being pushed back against the fridge, then the soft snick of the bolt being drawn.

A gray crack appeared along the wall as the door opened and she saw Jason silhouetted against the night sky.

Then his hand was on her arm and he pulled her through the doorway. Without giving herself a chance to think, she jumped down onto the graveled roof of the building next door, still clutching her envelope. She lost her balance and put out her hands to steady herself, scraping them on the gravel. Scrambling to her feet, she moved out of the way and rubbed her hands against her jeans to take some of the sting out.

The wind found her immediately, knifing through her clothes. She stuck the envelope inside her sweatshirt to keep from losing it and to cut down on the wind. From the roof she could see part of the alley on one side of the building and a brightly lit, empty street on the other side. Whoever had switched off the breaker was alone, or they were all in the building.

Jason closed the curtain, then jumped down too. He turned around and, leaning out precariously, gently closed the door. He stayed there, hands splayed against the closed door, until Laura grabbed him by the belt of his jeans and hauled.

"Thanks," he whispered when he was safely on the roof. "I can't believe we used to do that for fun."

Laura grinned at him. In spite of his short haircut and expensive sweater, he was still Jason, who could always turn calamity into adventure.

"Come on," she whispered. "We can take the truck."

"Whose truck is it?"

"Later," she replied. "It's a long story."

They walked in a crouch to the alley side of the building, then lay down flat to peer over the edge of the roof. From that vantage point they could clearly see the length of the alley between Tutshi Street and Duke. Laura noted the red dumpster with its open lid, the back of the white brick building on the other side of the alley, even the potholes that could swallow a small car. What she didn't see was the truck. She stuck a hand in her pocket and felt the hard outline of the truck keys.

"Where is it?" asked Jason.

Laura scooted back from the edge and sat up. Sharp stones dug through the tough fabric of her jeans to bite her tender flesh. She shivered as the wind found the gap between sweatshirt and jeans.

"It's gone," she replied. "Jason, I'm so sorry I got you into this!"

He inched his way back and sat up too. Then he slapped her shoulder playfully. "Don't start with me, Thorsen. You couldn't keep me away from a story this good. Come on, we have to get off this roof."

The neighboring building was three feet higher than the roof on which they stood, but since it abutted theirs, they were able to scramble onto it easily. There was still no sign of life from the newspaper office. The door to the darkroom stayed shut, and as there were no windows on that side of the building, they couldn't even tell if someone was wandering around with a flashlight.

It occurred to Laura that a short circuit might have caused the power outage. What if they were skulking around the roofs of Whitehorse because a mouse had nibbled through the wrong wire?

A car drove by.

"Now what?" said Laura, having inched her way to the far side of the building.

The next building over was too far and too low for them to jump. Besides, they would soon run out of buildings. If someone was looking for them in the newspaper office, it was only a matter of time before they found the darkroom door. She wanted to get down.

Jason had been examining the roof's edge. "Over here," he called softly. Laura ran over, shivering. A narrow metal ladder was latched to the brick wall on the alley side, leading to within six feet of the ground.

She closed her eyes, trying to decide if she could jump six feet without breaking a bone.

"Come on," said Jason, nudging her. "You go first."

With a muffled curse, she turned around and set foot gingerly on the first rung. When it didn't collapse, she tried the second one. By the time she was midway, Jason had stepped on the first rung. As he swung his foot down again, something pinged on the cement ledge next to the ladder. Jason started and looked around the roof.

"Get down, you idiot!" shouted Laura when she realized what was happening. Jason ducked below the roofline just as another bullet pinged past where he'd been standing.

"Jesus!" he cried, practically sliding down the ladder, "they're shooting at us!"

Laura reached the final rung and flung herself into empty air. She landed in a crouch with a jarring thud, lost her balance and rocked onto her hams just as Jason landed next to her. He lost his balance, too, and fell on top of her. After a mad scramble of limbs, they disentangled themselves and rose to their feet.

"Let's go!" cried Jason. They ran down the alley, heading for Tutshi Street as fast as they could.

A shout behind them warned them they'd been seen. Something kicked up asphalt at their feet. The gunman was using a silencer.

"Don't stop!" called Laura. They emerged onto the street and turned right, toward the more populated restaurant and movie district. The sound of feet pounding in the alley behind them spurred them on.

The envelope in her waistband worked its way free and Laura clutched it against her body as she ran. Her feet hit the asphalt like a hand slapping a cheek. Jason kept pace with her, although he was breathing hard. Something whizzed above her head and she automatically hunched her shoulders, expecting a bullet in her back.

"We have to split up," she gasped as they turned yet another corner in an effort to elude their pursuers.

"Go…police!" Jason's words came out staccato.

"No!" She grabbed his hand, ducked into an alley and pulled him into a recessed doorway about halfway down. "No police," she whispered, trying to get her breathing under control. Next to her, Jason breathed like a bellows, and she wished he could be quieter.

Then she placed her hand over his mouth and he nodded. Running footsteps came nearer as their pursuer approached the alley. He paused at the mouth of the alley, and Laura controlled an impulse to peek and see who it was. Apparently satisfied that the alley was empty, the pursuer began running again.

Jason relaxed and would have spoken, but Laura kept her hand on his mouth. A soft scrape at the other end of the alley told them someone else was listening. After a long time they heard the regular thud of someone in soft shoes running away from them.

Only then did Laura remove her hand.

"Why not the cops?" demanded Jason in a barely audible whisper.

"Could be on the take." At his skeptical snort she elaborated. "Tucker's got informants everywhere."

It was dark in the alley. The light from street lamps on the streets at either end didn't reach this far in. Laura couldn't see his face, but she could well imagine it. "I'm so sorry, Jase."

After a moment he shook his head. "Don't sweat it, Laura. But you're right—we have to split up. I don't think we should meet again until we're sure the story is out. Can I keep the flash drive?"

"Why?"

"Internet."

"How? You can't just walk into an internet café…"

"If you don't know where I'm going, you can't tell anyone else."

Laura shut her mouth and nodded. She had a hard copy of the article hidden in Fay's house. "Go for it, tiger."

"Where are you going to go?" he asked.

"If you don't know…" she began, and grinned when he poked her in the ribs.

"Okay, smart ass. You ready?"

She wasn't. The last thing she wanted to do was step out of the alley and expose herself to two hired killers. But Jason seemed to think she was braver than she actually was, and she'd be damned if she'd disappoint him. Especially now that she'd dragged him into this mess.

"Let's go," she whispered.

They left the protection of the doorway and stepped into the alley. Without a word, Jason turned left and walked away. She watched him for a moment, wishing safety on him. Then she turned right and headed for the street.

She was only a few blocks from the movie theater. Even on a Thursday night there'd be people on Main Street, going in and out of bars and restaurants, heading for the bookstore, coming out of the movies. She'd be safer there.

Where the *hell* was Mack's truck?

As she approached the well-lit street, her steps became more hesitant. She didn't want to leave the alley. But she couldn't stay here all night—she had to get home to Fay. Besides, the alley wasn't safe. When they didn't find her and Jason, the killers would double back.

Flattening herself against the wall of the building, Laura listened. All she could hear was the distant sound of a truck a couple of streets over. Taking a deep breath, she stepped onto the sidewalk.

"Got you!" growled a man behind her, and a heavy hand grabbed her arm.

Terror switched on her adrenaline and cleared her mind. Instead of pulling away from him, she stepped into him, jabbing his instep as hard as she could with the heel of her running shoe and slamming her head back. She connected with his nose.

"You bitch!" screamed her assailant, and she whirled out of his slackened grip. She caught a glimpse of a bald, shining head and blood gushing out of a nose, and then she was running.

Her mind screamed at her to zigzag, but her body ran in a straight line as hard and as fast as she could. Something tugged at her sleeve, but she couldn't spare any attention to it.

Main Street was only four blocks away. Already she could see people on the side streets. A couple stood under the streetlight of one side street, laughing. A car drove by on another.

She wanted to scream, but needed all her breath for running. The man behind her was running faster mad than she was scared. At this rate he would catch her before she could reach the main drag.

Surely someone could see her? Had Whitehorse become so big that a woman running from a bleeding thug raised no eyebrows?

Two blocks to go. Her pounding feet hit the street just as a battered orange pickup pulled up to her in a screech of brakes.

"Get in!" yelled Mack, leaning over to open the door for her.

She dove into the passenger side and he pulled away. Sitting up, she hung out the doorway and pulled the door shut. Only then did she look out the back window.

The bald, bleeding man stood in the middle of the road, taking aim at the truck with an amazingly long pistol.

"Duck!" she screamed.

The back window shattered in an explosion of safety glass.

"You son of a bitch!" yelled Mack. He turned onto a side street and sped away before the man could get another shot off.

Laura twisted to look out the back window. Cold air rushed inside the cab, freezing her cheeks, making her shiver. There was no sign of the shooter. There was no sign of anybody. Then Mack turned onto well-lit

Fourth Avenue, heading for the highway.

"No," she said, then repeated it louder to be heard over the sounds of the truck engine and the wind rushing in. "We have to find Jason!"

Mack glanced in the rearview mirror. The lines around his mouth were etched deep. His hands clamped tightly on the steering wheel, as if he was afraid to lose control of the truck. "Who the hell is Jason?"

"My friend." When Mack kept driving, she put a hand on his arm to make him understand. "Mack! He's running from them, too, and it's my fault. We can't leave him."

She shivered again. She was very cold now.

"All right! Where is he?"

Laura looked out the windshield. Where was Jason?

"Where is he, Laura?" asked Mack again.

"I…I'm not sure," she finally admitted. Her body was beginning to shake from the cold. "He wouldn't tell me where he was going, just in case."

Somewhere along the way she had managed to get her sleeve wet, maybe from a puddle on a roof, and now the cold air was freezing it to her arm. She wrapped her arms around herself, trying to warm up, and winced at a twinge in her shoulder.

"So what do you propose we do?" asked Mack angrily. "Drive around the streets looking for him? How do you figure we avoid the guy with the gun?"

Two guys, actually, thought Laura fuzzily. The cold was starting to get to her. She couldn't seem to think straight anymore.

"What's the matter?" asked Mack with sudden concern. The noise level dropped as the truck slowed down and Mack turned to take a good look at her. "Oh, Jesus," he said. "You've been shot."

Astonished, Laura looked down at herself. Her left sleeve was soaked, not with water, but with blood.

CHAPTER EIGHT

Fay was dreaming. She knew she was dreaming because she was happy. Sawyer was sitting on the porch of the old cabin, one step up from her, combing out her long hair. Her arms rested on his knees as he gently pulled apart knots until her hair was shiny and smooth. They were laughing.

Fay gradually became aware that she was still sitting in the straight-back chair by the woodstove. She had fallen asleep with her hands clasped over her belly, like an old woman.

Still warm and happy from the dream, she opened her eyes. Sawyer stood before her, smiling tenderly.

"Oh, beloved," she whispered.

The sound of a truck coming down the driveway intruded and she glanced toward the door. When she looked back, Sawyer was gone.

With a deep sigh Fay reached down and picked up the 12-gauge Remington from the floor. She flipped off the safety catch, then switched off the lamp and stood up.

Maybe she was seeing ghosts because she was about to die.

The door at the far end of the basement opened, letting in a gust of cold night air.

"Fay?" called Mack. "I need help here."

She flipped the safety back on the shotgun, set it down and turned the light on. Mack stood framed in the doorway, his arm around her daughter.

"What happened?" demanded Fay, hurrying over as he led Laura inside.

Laura's face was too pale.

"I'm okay," said Laura. "It looks worse than it is."

Then Fay saw the bloodstained rag around her daughter's left shoulder. "Dear God," she whispered, and promptly put aside her emotions to let the nurse in her take over.

They sat Laura down at the kitchen table, then Fay gently untied the makeshift bandage and pulled Laura's oversized sweatshirt off. The T-shirt beneath it was soaked with blood all down one side. Laura hissed when Fay peeled the sleeve away from her seeping wound, but didn't say a word.

"The people who did this," said Fay to the room in general, "are they likely to come here?"

"We weren't followed," said Mack, rummaging around the piled equipment in the corner of the basement.

"What about Hicklin?" asked Laura.

"Who's Hicklin?" said Mack.

Laura kept her gaze firmly on Mack as Fay tried to get a better look at the wound. "Blond ponytail at the gas station."

Mack grinned over his shoulder at her. "I hope he filled up, 'cause I sent him to Teslin."

Laura grinned too, but it was a weak one. Teslin was two hours south of Whitehorse, on the way to British Columbia. It would be a while before he made it back.

Mack returned with a large rubber container that held everything from disinfectant to splints. Fay stared at him.

He shrugged. "I like to be prepared."

"Go heat some water." Fay's words came out as an order when she had meant to request, but Mack didn't seem to mind. He nodded and filled a kettle from the laundry sink.

She found a pair of scissors in the container and cut away the sleeve and shoulder seam of Laura's T-shirt. "Who's Hicklin?" she asked, repeating Mack's question.

"Johnny T.'s man." Laura cleared her throat. "I recognized him when we stopped to get gas."

Mack turned away from the tap to look at them. "This place is hard to find in broad daylight, let alone in the middle of the night," he said. "We're safe, but I'll stand watch anyway."

Fay nodded, as if his saying they were safe made it so. This Johnny T. had found her daughter. She looked at Laura's shoulder and her stomach did a slow flip. To her relief, Laura was right. The wound wasn't as bad as it first seemed. A deep scratch in the meaty part of her shoulder had bled profusely. Fay hadn't seen one since her nursing days in Vancouver, but she still knew a bullet graze when she saw one.

"How did you get this bullet wound?"

Laura glanced at Mack before looking at Fay.

They've formed a bond, Fay realized, and the thought warmed her.

They told her what had happened in town and the warmth evaporated. She was going to have to convince Laura to go to the police.

She checked the expiration date on the disinfectant and poured it liberally on the three-inch groove.

Laura jumped and yelped. "Jesus!" She yanked her arm away. "That hurts!"

"Good," snapped Fay. "Next time don't get shot." She dabbed the wound dry and laced it with an antibiotic ointment. Then she placed a sterile pad over it and wrapped a gauze strip securely around Laura's arm and shoulder. "You'll have a nice scar to show my grandchildren if you don't get yourself killed first. Don't move it too much or it'll start bleeding again."

"Your concern is touching," said Laura tartly.

Mack plunked the teapot down in the middle of the table. "Will you two please stop?" he asked tightly. "Don't you have any idea how lucky you are to have each other?" He gave them a reproachful look and went out, closing the door firmly behind him.

Fay and Laura stared at the closed door.

"What's the matter with him?" demanded Laura. "I'm the one who got shot."

The blood caking Laura's T-shirt looked black in the dim light of the overhead bulb. Fay wondered if Mack could spare a shirt. They weren't likely to get back to the house any time soon. "He has no family. Both his parents died when he was fourteen. He lived with foster families until he was old enough to go out on his own."

"Oh." Laura couldn't seem to find anything else to say.

Fay took a deep breath. Mack was right. Laura was all she had left. The bullet wound proved one thing—she could have lost her daughter tonight. She brushed at the dried blood on her hands, trying not to let the realization unravel her.

"Laura, I'm very sorry I said those things this morning."

Laura looked startled, and blushed. Her next words sent hope soaring through Fay.

"I'm sorry too," she said. "I hope you know it's not true." She looked directly at Fay. "I never once felt that the wrong parent had died."

Fay looked down at the tabletop, surprised by the sudden tears in her eyes. Laura's words relieved an ache that had lain within her since

James died. "You loved your dad very much. It would be perfectly understandable."

"Fay," said Laura, with a hint of her familiar asperity. "Dad died, and I miss him. That doesn't mean I wanted you dead instead of him."

Fay tamped down her usual irritation at Laura's tone. "Thank you," she said gravely.

It was a good start, and she was content with it. They were both tired, physically and emotionally, and Laura needed to recover from the shock of being shot. Tomorrow they could pursue this fragile new relationship they were building.

But Laura had other ideas.

"Since we're on the subject, and I don't mean to criticize or anything, but I need to know—were you jealous of me and Dad?"

Fay breathed deeply, trying to keep her blood pressure under control. Laura had never been tactful, and didn't understand the concept of leaving well enough alone. Perhaps that flaw made her a good reporter. It certainly made her an uncomfortable child to love.

She couldn't remember ever having a heart-to-heart talk with Laura. Now that the moment had arrived, she was amazed at how unpleasant it felt.

Keeping her voice steady, she replied. "I suppose I was jealous of you and your father at times. You were very close, and I sometimes felt excluded."

Laura's chin tilted and Fay almost winced. Wrong word.

"Excluded!" said Laura. "We *always* invited you! You hardly ever came. We didn't exclude you—you shut us out! Don't you think I would have liked to have my mother take an interest in my life?"

Heat rose in Fay's face and for a moment she wanted to shake her daughter.

"Did it never occur to you to wonder why?" Her throat felt too tight, her voice too sharp. "Your father tried very hard to distance you from me. He usurped all the fun things to do with you and left me with the discipline. He was always your accomplice. How many little secrets did the two of you share? Why did he plan special outings at times when I couldn't go? I was a nurse. I worked shifts. My days off rarely coincided with yours, and when they did, the two of you wanted to go climbing. He knew I was afraid of heights. Perhaps I wasn't the best mother for you, but your father didn't help."

She took a long shuddery breath, trying to regain control, and continued more quietly. "I'm not saying he did it on purpose, or even that he was aware of it, but your father was going to make sure you were on his side, no matter what happened between him and me."

A long, tense silence followed Fay's outburst. Laura stared at her, mouth slightly open.

Fay went to the counter where she found three cups. She returned to the table, poured tea into two of them and sat down. She ladled sugar into Laura's and pushed the cup at her daughter.

"Drink," she said.

* * *

Laura lay fully clothed next to Mack on the thick foam pad he used for a bed, staring into the darkness of the unfinished basement. He had lent her a clean sweatshirt that was much too big, but it was warm. In spite of the painkillers, her shoulder throbbed in time to her heartbeat. At least it was her left arm that was hurt.

Fay had taken first watch, striding out into the dark with the Remington and a flashlight. Laura suspected her mother had welcomed the chance to be alone.

Next to her, Mack slept, his breathing deep and regular. Laura was amazed at his ability to just blink out of awareness, in spite of everything that had happened. Even more amazing was that she was lying next to him, completely indifferent, when only hours ago he had filled her with longing.

But that was before someone shot at her, and before her version of the past went flying out the window.

Her mind skittered around Fay's revelations like a drop of water on a hot griddle. Which was worse—that her mother had felt left out of the family, or that Laura hadn't noticed? Had her father manipulated his only child's affections as insurance against loneliness?

Hadn't her parents loved each other?

Don't think about it now, she decided. *First survive, and then you can figure out how you could have been so blind all these years.*

Instead, her mind turned to Jason. Was he all right? Had he made it? If she didn't hear from him tomorrow, she would take her chances with the police. By then people would know about Johnny Tucker's crime network, even if the article didn't get through to the news service. The reporter in Vancouver would have her copy, and so would the attorney general. Tucker couldn't have his hooks in everybody!

Please be all right, Jase. Please be safe.

She had mishandled the whole affair, dragging Fay, Mack and Jason into a dangerous situation not of their making. All for what—a scoop? A professional coup? Her arrogance had endangered friends and family, and almost gotten her killed.

She relived her harrowing escape from the newspaper office, trying to control her shaking. If Mack hadn't been there…

He had hitchhiked into town after getting rid of Hicklin. It wasn't that the man had seemed threatening, but he had asked directions for Wild Rose Lane. That was when Mack had signaled her to take off. He sent Hicklin in the wrong direction, found someone going to town and ended up within six blocks of the newspaper office.

He found his truck in the alley. Then he saw two men picking the lock of the door in the alley. He tried to follow them in, but the door locked behind them.

He considered breaking the window to warn her—if she was there—but as he was looking for a rock, the lights went out inside the building. He immediately fished the spare key from its magnetic holder inside the front bumper and drove around to the front of the building, hoping Laura would see him and come out. When nothing happened, he drove slowly around the block, wondering if she was still inside, if he should call the police or try to break in. Just as he was passing an alley, he glimpsed a woman running past the far end. Instinct made him floor the gas pedal and he reached her moments before the killer did.

Only grace and good fortune had kept her from being killed. Grace, good fortune and Mack. Her trembling increased and tears pricked her eyelids. She hoped Jason had been lucky, too. What was she doing? This was too big for her. Too big for any one person. She was going to have to take a chance on the police.

She turned onto her good side, away from Mack, stifling a groan as the movement jarred her shoulder. The tears spilled out onto the pillow and she opened her mouth to breathe more quietly.

In a rustle of movement, Mack slid an arm under her neck. He nestled her back against his chest and wrapped his other arm gently around her belly, careful not to jostle her arm. She rested her head against his shoulder, comforted by his warm breath on her hair. Silent and warm, he held her as she wept until she finally fell asleep.

* * *

Laura stared up at the sky, shivering in the ghostly half-light of dawn. One by one, the stars paled and winked out of existence.

She felt on the verge of winking out of existence herself. Her mouth was dry and gummy, her nose was plugged, and she had a headache. No wonder she hated crying.

She also hated outhouses, especially on cold mornings when a rim of frost circled the seat. She rubbed her bum with her good hand, trying to restore circulation. Mack and Fay had let her sleep the rest of the night. She wished she felt better for it.

She rotated her shoulder gingerly and was rewarded with an increased range of movement. It still hurt, but it was bearable. The rest had done some good, apparently.

It was a clear morning, and her cheeks tingled with the cold. She took a deep breath, trying to clear the cobwebs from her head.

Hugging her injured arm to her body, she wandered back to the unfinished house. Her feet crunched through wild grass made brittle by the frost. A week ago, nothing but Paris would have satisfied her. Now all she wanted was a bath, clean clothes and warmth. She could just imagine how Mack and Fay felt. It was time to end this nightmare—as soon as Mack and Fay showed up, they would go to the police.

Where were they? She had awakened to an empty basement and even her trip to the outhouse hadn't roused them. She had assumed they were walking around the grounds, but surely…

"Good morning," said Fay, stepping out of the trees.

Laura started, and she winced at the pain the sudden movement caused. "Good morning yourself," she said as cheerfully as she could manage. "Where's Mack?"

"Down the driveway," said Fay. She wore a man's heavy sweater with the sleeves rolled down to keep her hands warm. The shotgun was cradled casually in one arm.

She looks so tired, thought Laura with a stab of guilt.

"Did you get any sleep at all?" she asked her mother.

Fay shook her head. "I tried, but you were snoring too much."

Mortified, Laura was about to apologize when she caught her mother's sly sideways glance.

Laura laughed.

Fay grinned. "I'm hungry. Want some breakfast?"

At the mention of food, Laura's stomach growled. When had she last eaten? "Sounds good to me."

They turned companionably toward the house. As they passed by the dark hulk of the pickup, parked next to the entrance, Laura suddenly remembered the envelope with the two pictures.

"Hold on," she told her mother. "There's something I want you to see."

Fay obediently stopped and watched as Laura opened the door to the cab. The interior light came on.

"Come over to the light," said Laura, sweeping safety glass off the seat. She pulled the photographs out of the envelope and handed her mother the snapshot. "Who's the man on the top step?" she asked. "He looks like the man I saw in the woods yesterday."

Fay put down the rifle on the truck seat and took the snapshot from Laura. She stared at it for a long time. Finally she said, in a voice barely above a whisper, "He was a friend of ours, before you came along. You couldn't have seen him, dear."

Laura studied the picture again. "I know it couldn't have been him—this picture is over thirty years old—but still...I could have sworn..."

Then Fay saw the other picture. "When did you get this done?" she asked, reaching for the picture of the grim-faced Aunt Gertrude.

"That's not me." Laura grinned. She took the picture from her mother and flipped it over. "Apparently it's Great Aunt Gertrude. Or maybe Great Great... I get lost in too many *greats*."

Fay frowned and took the picture again. She looked at the handwriting on the back, and even in the poor light of the cab, Laura saw her pale.

"Where did you get it?" asked Fay. Her lips looked almost gray and Laura took her arm in concern.

"Mom? What's the matter?" She tried to take the picture from Fay but her mother's hand clenched on it spasmodically.

"Where did you get it?" repeated Fay, enunciating very clearly.

Laura's heart hammered in her chest. She had triggered something, but she didn't know what. Her mother looked like she was in shock. Not knowing what else to do, Laura told her the truth.

"At the *Trib* office. Jason said Dad had given both pictures to Mr. Howell to give to me when he died. Dad, I mean." At her mother's blank look Laura took a deep breath and tried again. "Dad gave them to Mr. Howell. Mr. Howell was supposed to give them to me if Dad died before him, but I guess Mr. Howell forgot."

Fay looked even worse. Her face was chalk white. Her free hand held on to the door frame as if for support. Alarmed, Laura stepped closer to her mother and took the pictures from her strengthless hand.

Through tight lips Fay asked, "When? When did James give them to Howell?"

For the first time in her life Laura felt the inexorable pull of destiny. Without understanding how, she knew her next words would change her life and her mother's, but she could no more have refrained from answering than she could have kept the sun from rising.

"Ten years ago," she said.

Fay's face went from chalk white to violent red. She stepped away from the truck, pulling out of Laura's embrace as if she didn't exist. In the growing light of day her eyes glittered with unshed tears.

"The son of a bitch," whispered Fay, stumbling drunkenly from the truck. She looked around at the gray trees. "You son of a bitch!" The tendons in her neck stood out with the force of her cry.

She turned her back to the house and broke into an awkward trot, heading for the cliff trail.

With a wordless cry of fear, Laura followed her mother.

CHAPTER NINE

Fay ran as fast as she could, rage fueling her legs and lungs. Her mind was too full of fury to form coherent thought and her entire being focused on only one goal: James.

She raced the half mile to her home, dimly aware of the cliff's edge, the slippery path, her laboring heart.

After what seemed like an eternity, she burst out of the trees into the cleared space surrounding her house and skidded to a stop. She struggled to catch her breath, inhaling raggedly through the pain in her side. The house she and James had built loomed darkly, sleepily, but she wasn't fooled.

"You knew!" she yelled at the quiet house when her heaving chest finally allowed. "All those *years* you knew!" A harsh sob escaped. "James!" She wiped at her face and turned around, examining the trees. "James, you bastard—come out!"

But James didn't appear. Instead, Laura came running up the path, holding her arm awkwardly. Two red splotches stood out on either cheek, made vivid by the pallor of her face.

"Fay," she gasped when she caught sight of her mother. She

stumbled to a stop. "What are you doing?"

Sanity came crashing back as Fay looked at her daughter. What *was* she doing, demanding an accounting of a ghost? If he hadn't had the decency to tell her as a living, breathing man, why did she think he would face her now?

"Who were you yelling at?" asked Laura, her tone partway between a plea and a demand.

She thinks I'm losing my mind, thought Fay. The sustaining rage and adrenaline suddenly deserted her and she swayed on trembling legs.

"Mom!" cried Laura, reaching for her mother, but Fay steadied herself and shook her head. Somewhere deep inside, she realized that her daughter had just called her Mom. Again.

"I'm fine, Laura." She tried a smile. "I'm all right."

Laura shook her head, her expression grim, and with a feeling somewhere between relief and trepidation, Fay knew it was time to tell her daughter the truth. But before she could put order in her thoughts, Laura continued.

"Mom," said Laura, "were you calling *Dad?*"

Before Fay could answer, a voice spoke up.

"Hello, Laura."

* * *

Fear clawed at Laura's throat and both women whirled toward the house. For a moment Laura could only stare at the tall figure stepping out of the doorway. Then she took in the slim build, short, curly brown hair and blue eyes. Adam—it was Adam Rhys, her editor.

She got an impression of dark slacks and a black bomber jacket before her eyes focused on his eyes. She smiled tentatively, glad to see him in spite of everything.

"Adam? What are you doing here? How did you find me?"

He looked at her, shaking his head. "You're so damned secretive.

No friends to speak of, no phone calls home on the company phone. Nothing. But you named your mother as beneficiary on the magazine's insurance plan."

Laura closed her eyes briefly. Undone by bureaucracy. Was that how Johnny T. had found her?

Adam came down a step, keeping his hands in his jacket pockets against the morning chill. He was smiling. He looked around at the forest and the cliff only a few dozen feet away, the ribbon of river glinting in the increasing light. He turned to Fay and raised his voice slightly.

"This is a beautiful spot, Mrs. Thorsen. And you have a beautiful home. I hope you don't mind that I waited inside—it was very cold last night and the door was unlocked."

Fay glanced at Laura but didn't say a word. Laura looked around the house, searching for a vehicle, but there was nowhere to hide one. "What are you doing here, Adam?" she asked again.

Adam sighed. "I've come to talk sense into you." He shook his head and she thought she detected a genuine sadness in his eyes. "I told you to drop the story. You said you would. But you had to go ahead anyway, didn't you?"

"Why didn't you publish it?" she demanded, stepping closer, placing herself between Fay and Adam. He was acting strange. Stiff. As though he didn't want to be here.

"Tucker's men are in town now," she said. "They tried to kill me last night."

Adam looked startled. "I thought I'd have more time…"

"Time for what, Adam?" Laura stared at him. "All you had to do was publish the article, an article that would have made both our careers. Why didn't you?"

"Because he works for Mr. Tucker," said Fay flatly, startling them both. Laura glanced at her mother, then turned back to Adam, expecting a hot denial. When he stayed silent, dread pooled in her stomach.

"Adam?" she said softly. "Is it true?"

He smiled ruefully. "She's pretty perceptive, for a crazy person. I understand now why you never talk about her."

Laura winced but pursued her original question. "Is it true, Adam? Do you work for Johnny T.?"

He didn't reply.

Oh God. Adam.

"I needed money for Mom's treatments," he finally said. "There was an experimental treatment in the States, but it cost so much…"

Laura took a deep breath. "Your mother died three years ago."

He smiled sadly. "It was too late by then."

"So you sold my daughter out?" demanded Fay. She put a hand on Laura's good shoulder. It trembled. Laura couldn't tell if it was out of fear or rage.

Adam shook his head vehemently. "I'm trying to *save* your daughter," he said. He shifted his gaze to Laura. "I've come to take you back with me. You have to convince Johnny that you'll keep quiet. It's your only chance."

He really believes that, thought Laura wonderingly. She was intensely aware of her mother standing silently behind her. What was Fay thinking?

"Adam, did you bring those men here?" she asked.

He shook his head. "No," he said firmly. He took a deep breath of the cold morning air.

When he didn't elaborate, Laura knew. "But you told Johnny T. where to find me." She suddenly wanted to grab Fay's hand and run. She glanced around the trees surrounding the house. Were Johnny T.'s goons even now closing in?

She suddenly remembered Mack. She had to warn him…

"She can't go back," said Fay. "Your friend will kill her, no matter what you think." Fay's voice was hard and Laura turned to look at her. Her mother's expression was furious.

Adam's hands emerged from his pockets to wave away Fay's suggestion.

"No! He promised. If we can persuade him she'll stay quiet…"

He looked stricken suddenly and Laura knew what he was thinking.

"That's right," she said. "It's not just me anymore, is it?" She took a deep, shuddering breath. "It's Fay. Johnny Tucker will never let us walk away alive."

Adam shook his head. "You have to convince him you'll both keep your mouths shut. If you do, he'll leave you alone."

Laura stared at him for a long moment. "Sure. That's why his men were shooting at me."

He shook his head. "That was just a misunderstanding. Come with me—"

Now it was Laura's turn to be furious. This man had been her friend. They had almost been lovers. And he had betrayed her. Not only had he put her life in jeopardy, he had put her mother's life at risk, too. And Mack's. And Jason's.

"You'll forgive me for doubting his good faith, if not yours," she said acidly. She tilted her chin up at him. "You'd better get out of here, Adam. I'm calling the cops."

Adam looked down at her. Emotions flitted across his face, finally settling on resignation. "You'll do it, won't you?" he said softly.

Before Laura could nod in agreement, he pulled a pistol out of his pocket and pointed it at her.

Without thinking, Laura pulled her mother behind her.

"I'm sorry, Laura," said Adam, "but you *are* coming with me."

Fay put a trembling hand on Laura's back. "Does this man pay you well enough to kill for him?" she asked.

"Nobody's going to get killed," said Adam.

A cool breeze kissed Laura's cheeks. She stared at the pistol in Adam's hand and found nothing to say. In the canyon the river rumbled its approval of the approaching day. Even the pines seemed more fragrant than usual.

"If nobody's going to get killed," said Fay, "why are you pointing a gun at us?"

Adam looked down at his hand as if it didn't belong to him. He ignored Fay completely, and it seemed to Laura that her mother made him uneasy. She thought of what had happened earlier as it must have appeared to him—Fay bursting into the clearing and shouting at the house like a madwoman.

He thinks she's insane. Maybe he's right.

"You know, Laura," said Adam, "I am trying to help you. The bomb in your car should have killed you. Right now I'm your only chance."

Out of the corner of her eye Laura saw Fay start at the mention of the bomb. She hadn't told her mother about it. There was a lot she hadn't told her mother.

She swallowed the unexpected grief and concentrated on the problem facing her. What exactly did Adam intend to do? Surely he couldn't mean to shoot them. Two women dead of bullet wounds would raise a few eyebrows—something Johnny T. wanted to avoid.

Adam sighed and finally descended the porch steps. Laura watched his approach warily, but she refused to back away. He stopped out of easy reach, and determination replaced regret in his expression.

"Nobody thought you'd come back to the house, but they left me here, just in case. You're lucky it was me. They'll listen to me. You have two choices—keep running and die, or come with me and live."

Laura wasn't even tempted to believe him. He could fool himself if it made him feel better, but the man who shot her last night hadn't wanted to persuade her. He had wanted her dead.

No matter what Adam thought, Johnny Tucker didn't leave loose ends. And Laura would be a loose end. So would Fay. And Mack, too, if they learned about him.

"It's too late, Adam," said Laura slowly. "The story's out. It's with the RCMP and the Attorney General's office. But it's not too late for you. Help me. Don't let filth like Tucker bring you down."

Adam shook his head reluctantly. "Nice try, Laura, but I don't believe you. You want this scoop too much. You wouldn't share it with anyone—it would steal your glory."

Laura didn't dare look at her mother. She was smarter than he gave her credit for, but just as greedy. How could she convince him of the truth?

Adam gestured with the pistol. "Turn around, both of you. We're going to walk down the driveway to where I left the jeep. And Laura, please don't try anything. You probably think I won't dare shoot, but I will if I have to. I know you don't believe this, but I really am on your side."

Laura didn't move. "I'll go with you, but leave my mother out of it. She doesn't know what's going on. You saw her just now. She's no danger to you." If he thought she was crazy...

Adam was already shaking his head. "You know better than that. You'll both have to come." He stepped forward and Laura's legs trembled with the urge to rush him. He wouldn't shoot. They'd shared too much for too long— they'd gotten drunk on scotch together and almost slept together. Could he really bring himself to pull the trigger?

The impulse passed. Had she been alone with him, she might have tried it.

She turned around and faced her mother. Fay's cheeks were rosy, and Laura couldn't tell if that was from emotion, or from the exertion of her recent run. They stared at each other for a long moment. Laura couldn't read her mother's expression. Was she all right?

Laura tried a reassuring smile, but she knew it fell short when her mother frowned. Without a word Fay turned around and Adam shepherded them toward the driveway. They crunched through the gravel, their bodies casting long shadows before them.

"It'll be okay, Laura," said Adam, almost to himself. "Don't worry, I won't let them hurt you."

Just as he finished speaking, half a dozen wild swans glided silently down the river canyon, even with the top of the cliff. They came abreast of the three people and suddenly called to each other, their haunting cries sounding like lost souls. Startled, Adam turned to look at the creatures.

Laura grabbed Fay by the hand, whispered "Now!" and broke into a run. To her relief, Fay didn't hesitate but ran as fast as she could toward the trees. They ignored Adam's frantic calls for them to stop. Reaching the cover of the trees, they released each other and used their hands to protect their eyes from branches.

Something smacked into a tree next to Laura, immediately followed by a loud popping sound. A split second later she realized Adam was shooting at them. So much for sharing scotch.

The trees slowed them down too much. At this rate he was bound to hit one of them.

"Go for the trail," she told Fay, and they cut across the woods, heading for the cliff trail. It faithfully followed the cliff's rugged outline and would place them out of Adam's line of sight most of the time.

Within seconds, they broke out of the trees. Another shot rang out, echoing against the cliffs, but Laura couldn't tell where it hit.

A parade of curses marched through her mind like a mantra, but she didn't waste her breath voicing them. Fay ran ahead, heading for the highway a few miles away. Her pace was already slowing. She had run half a mile at full speed less than half an hour ago—how long before her body gave out?

Laura risked a glance behind her. Adam was close, too close. But as long as he was running, he couldn't aim.

They were nearing the side trail to the old cabin. Spurred by fear, Laura sprinted to join her mother.

"Go to the cabin," she directed, panting, when she had her mother's attention. Fay's flushed face didn't look good. She wouldn't be able to keep this up very long. "You know where the trail is, but he won't see it," continued Laura. "I'll join you as soon as I lose him."

She didn't think she could outrun Adam, even without Fay to slow her down. He had run three marathons so far this year. She might outsprint him, but he could outlast her. Still, she had to get Fay out of danger, and this was the only idea she had.

Fay glanced back at her daughter, looking as if she wanted to say something, but she was breathing too hard to spare the breath. They rounded a curve and suddenly the side trail was there. Laura pushed her mother onto it, with a harsh, whispered, "Run!" Then she put on a burst of speed, catching up branches as she passed to make them swing and attract Adam's attention.

She looked back to make sure Fay was out of sight. To her horror, she saw her mother standing behind a tree by the curve of the trail, a sturdy branch held like a club in both hands.

"No!" she gasped, stumbling to a stop. Just then, Adam rounded the curve. He held the pistol in one relaxed hand and ran loosely, easily, as if he could do this all day.

Fay stepped out from behind the pine tree, startling him. She swung the branch and Adam reflexively raised the hand holding the pistol to deflect the blow just as his free hand reached out to grab the branch. A shot rang out and Fay spun away in a graceful pirouette, only to crumple to the ground.

"No!" screamed Laura, breaking into a run. "Mom!"

She had time to glimpse Adam's stricken expression, and then a madman came barreling out of the trees, roaring at the top of his lungs. In the split second it took Laura to recognize Mack, Adam swung the branch he was now holding in a wide arc that ended in a sickening crack against the side of Mack's head.

Momentum carried Laura past the terror. She was now so close that Adam couldn't have missed, but he was watching Mack, who was trying to get up despite the blood pouring from his scalp. Laura ran past her mother's crumpled body, not daring to look, and launched herself at Adam's back.

He had enough warning to whirl around and raise his arms, but he couldn't aim and Laura landed with her full weight against him. The pistol flew out of his hand as he lurched back, mouth parted in a grimace. Laura shrieked like a banshee, letting loose the fear and rage that had accumulated since the day her car blew up. She raised her hands to claw at his face, lusting for the feel of his flesh ripping under her nails.

He took one look at her expression and swung out wildly with his fist. Laura had enough presence of mind to turn her face and avoid a broken nose, but his fist landed on her right cheekbone, stunning her with pain. She reeled back and slipped on a rock made slick by a thin layer of ice.

Her legs swept out from under her and she twisted to land on her good side. As she did, her foot hooked between Adam's legs, sending him stumbling back, his arms waving wildly in an effort to retain his balance.

The landing knocked the breath out of her, but she scrambled to her feet within seconds, ready to attack again. She wheeled toward him, hands out to ward off the blows.

He wasn't there.

She turned quickly, certain he had circled behind her, but there was no one there. She glanced up and down the trail. No one. Finally, reluctantly, she stepped to the cliff's edge and looked down.

The sun had cleared the ridge of mountains and light flooded the river valley in rich hues of gold and pink, revealing Adam sprawled on his back on a stone outcropping, twenty feet from the top of the cliff. His leg was obviously broken, and his head was tucked into his shoulder, as if he had fallen asleep.

CHAPTER TEN

How is he?" asked Fay.

Laura looked up from bandaging Mack's bloody head to find her mother staring down at them. Her face was gray and she cradled her injured arm in the sling Laura had fashioned from the first aid supplies. The bullet was still lodged in Fay's upper arm, and Laura suspected the bone was broken, but aside from letting Laura bandage it, Fay was being stubborn about accepting help.

"For Christ's sake, Mom—at least sit down!" Laura stood up, took her mother by the arm and gently pushed her down to sit against the tree, next to Mack.

"*He* is fine," said Mack pointedly. His face was covered in drying blood, but underneath it, he was pale. Laura crouched next to him and finished tying the bandage as best she could. Then she examined the result. It looked as if someone wearing thick mittens had done the job. Not bad, considering how much she was shaking.

"We have to get you two to a hospital," she said. As instructed by Fay, she studied Mack's eyes for uneven pupil dilation. Both blue eyes stared back evenly, and she patted his stubbled cheek. Flakes of blood drifted off.

"First we have to see if your friend Adam is alive," said Fay.

Laura sat back on her heels and sighed. Her own shoulder burned with pain. She was sure it had started bleeding again but she couldn't spare the time to look. She had run back to the house for the first aid kit—nowhere near as elaborate as Mack's, but sufficient—and run back. Now she felt lightheaded and weak. She couldn't decide if she needed a stiff drink or a steak.

She wanted to call the police, but it would take half an hour for them to get here, longer if they couldn't find the road right away. The same for the ambulance. It would be faster if she drove Mack and Fay to the hospital and called the police from town.

Stifling a groan, she pushed herself upright. "Let's go. You both need more help than I can give you."

"We have to see if he's alive," repeated Fay firmly.

Anger rushed through Laura, lending her unexpected strength.

"That son of a bitch tried to kill us," she said bitterly. "I don't care if he's dead or alive."

Fay only looked more tired. "I do."

Mack struggled to his feet. "I'll go down," he said. "We can't leave him there—the ravens will get to him."

"None of us is in any shape to haul him up!" snapped Laura.

She took a deep, shuddering breath and tried to steady herself against the picture Mack had planted in her mind. Then she closed her eyes in defeat. They were right. They had to know if Adam was dead or alive. Her impulse was to leave him there to rot, but that would make her no better than the people Johnny Tucker hired.

If Adam was alive, someone would have to stay with him. If he was dead…

"Damn," she muttered. "I'll climb down."

Mack opened his mouth to argue and she cut him off. "You were hit over the head, Mack. Do you honestly think I'd let you climb down a cliff?"

"What about you?" he retorted. "You've got a bum shoulder—you're in no shape either."

"Trust me," she said grimly. "I can climb down and back." She had very little patience for male ego right now.

"Let her," said Fay. She looked up at the two of them from her spot at the base of the tree, and Laura realized she would have to hurry. Her mother looked worse now than a few minutes ago.

"She knows what she's doing, Mack," continued Fay. "She's had a lot of experience."

Laura noted the vote of confidence wryly. "Did you get rid of Dad's climbing equipment?" she asked.

Fay shook her head. "No, it's still in the garage." She told Laura exactly where to find it.

"Stay away from the edge of the cliff, both of you," warned Laura, and for the third time that morning, she ran to the house. She didn't even bother holding her arm this time, riding out the pain that had become her constant companion. She wondered if her shoulder would impede her climb, then decided to worry about it later. First she had to find the equipment.

The sun felt wonderful on her face and she made a mental note to bring back blankets for her mother and Mack. Warmth was necessary to ward off shock.

As she ran, she looked down at the river coursing turbulently a hundred feet below her. She had climbed up and down this particular cliff dozens of times with her father, practicing rappelling techniques. A sore shoulder shouldn't hamper her, even if it had been years since she last put on a harness.

For the first time since Adam appeared so suddenly on her mother's

121

porch, tension ebbed from Laura's muscles. She was alive. Her mother was alive, and so was Mack. They were all right.

Then, at her body's urgent warning, she stepped off the trail and threw up. She retched dryly until her sides ached. By the time she finally stopped, she was trembling with reaction.

When she arrived at the house, she grabbed a couple of blankets and some water. She didn't look around the house. She didn't want to see evidence of Adam's presence in her home.

In the garage she found the climbing equipment stored neatly in a labeled box and unceremoniously dumped it onto the cement floor. She picked through the contents, pulling out a sling and a couple of snap links which she stuffed into her jeans pockets.

She found a multi-colored nylon rope looped over a peg on the wall. Pulling it off, she stuck her head through the loop and settled the rope diagonally against shoulder and hip. As she gathered up the blankets and bottle, she realized she hadn't even considered calling an ambulance for Adam. He was dead, she was sure of it.

But what if he wasn't? She couldn't stay with him until an ambulance came… She had to get Fay and Mack to the hospital as soon as possible. Her mother would resist leaving if she thought Adam needed help and Laura didn't want to force a wounded, recalcitrant Fay to leave. Better to climb down, if only to humor Fay.

And if she found Adam still breathing? She would lie. She wasn't going to risk losing Fay for Adam.

Then the memory of their one kiss imposed itself, and she almost snarled in frustration. She marched back to the house where she dialed the emergency number and in short, succinct sentences, told the startled operator exactly where to find Adam. She even gave detailed directions, with no hope that they would help the ambulance driver arrive faster. She hung up, cutting off the operator's request for more information.

Mack stood up as soon as he saw her, and after taking a blanket from her, he tucked it around Fay. He used the other one to cradle her head against the tree. Then he held the water bottle to Fay's mouth while she drank. Fay rewarded him with a weak smile, and Laura felt her heart contract. Ten minutes. That's all she would take.

Without a word she removed the rope, the sling and the snap links, setting them carefully on the ground at her feet. Casting around, she finally decided on the stump of a black spruce tree that had been felled by lightning when she was a child. It was a bit far from the edge of the cliff, but she thought the rope would be long enough. When Mack saw the stump she had chosen, he checked to make sure he couldn't topple it. It didn't budge.

Laura found the two ends of the rope and from there the center. This she wrapped around the stump. Then she threaded one end of the rope through the sling, pulling the sling close to the stump. Holding the rope taut and even, she flung the ends over the edge of the cliff.

The colored rope pooled on the outcropping, contrasting sharply with the rusty rock. She dragged her gaze away from the sprawled body of her former boss and walked back to where she had left the sling. This she slipped through the snap link, centering it.

Aware of her mother's worried gaze, Laura stepped into the two loops and pulled the snap link up, adjusting the sling around her thighs. When she was comfortable, she formed a loop around her right thigh with the right hand rope, which was already threaded through the sling. This rope would act as a brake as she rappelled down. The left rope would steady her as she made her way down the cliff.

Without giving herself time to think, she walked backward toward the cliff.

"Wait a minute," objected Mack, putting a hand on her good arm to stop her. "Are you crazy? You'll end up just like him!" He nodded at

Adam. "At least tie the rope around yourself!"

Laura raised an eyebrow in amusement and even Fay smiled faintly. It did look dangerous to the uninitiated, but it was a fast, safe way to descend.

She freed one hand. "You're a nice man, Emmett," she said, patting his shoulder. "And I'm going to do my very best to make this whole mess up to you. But we're wasting time."

Mack looked frustrated, but he stepped back. She studied his face a moment longer. He looked drawn and tense. He probably had the grandfather of all headaches.

With both of them watching her, she didn't dare show her trepidation, but she had to steel herself for that first step off the cliff. It sloped sharply down to the water, with lots of crevices and outcroppings, but there was a relatively smooth way down and it was only twenty feet. She wished it hadn't been five years since she'd done any climbing.

With her left hand loose around the rope, she stepped off the cliff.

The moment she was in motion, her confidence returned. Her legs flexed slightly to absorb the shock. Her right hand controlled the speed of descent with minimal strength and she found she could ignore the pain in her left shoulder as she used the rope to steady herself. Within seconds she landed on the outcropping and freed herself from the sling.

Just like riding a bicycle.

The outcropping was fairly large, one of many studding the cliff as erosion did its uneven work. It was made out of clay and rock, and every year the river and the wind wore it down a bit more.

She looked up. There, framed by the trees, was Mack, staring down at her. He looked impressed. Standing behind him was Fay. She looked sick.

"Mother," said Laura calmly. "If you don't sit down right now, I will come back up and make you."

Mack looked around, saw Fay and led her away.

Finally Laura turned to Adam. He lay only a few feet away, unnaturally still. The moment she looked at him, she knew he was dead. Just as an empty house held a peculiar silence, so did an empty body. Nevertheless, she knelt by his side and felt for a pulse in his carotid artery. Nothing. Then she noticed the side of his head, where it rested on the outcropping, was oddly flat. She stood up quickly.

"He's dead," she called up to Mack, who had reappeared. She looked at the body again. In spite of her anger at Adam, his death called up an echo of grief. She had liked him.

"Send down a blanket," she told Mack.

He nodded and pulled up the rope. He tied one end around a blanket. "Stand back," he said and tossed it down. It landed cleanly at her feet. Laura untied the woolen blanket and held it against her chest. She would have to tuck it under him, at the very least.

She had to straighten his legs and almost cried out when she felt the bones in his broken leg shift against each other. Swallowing her horror, she shrouded the body as best she could.

When she was finished, she stood up and walked the few feet to the edge of the outcropping. She stared down the river valley for a long minute, trying to control her breathing. The sun glinted off the water and turned the sides of the cliffs a rich terra cotta. Two pintail ducks winged their way up the river, their feathers shimmering like emeralds. The breeze brought the scent of wood smoke. The whole world seemed peaceful.

"Laura," called Mack. "It's time to go."

She looked over her shoulder at him and nodded. "Right." With a last glance at Adam's body she reached for the rope.

"Do you want me to tie the rope around the stump?" asked Mack.

Laura examined the path she would take up the cliff. Crevices seamed the cliff like long skinny fingers splayed against a wall. Poplar bushes and the odd, crazy-angled evergreen dotted the numerous outcroppings. It would be easy enough to walk up the cliff, but she didn't want to take a chance with her shoulder.

"Yes," she called up. He nodded and disappeared, only to return moments later.

"Okay," he said. "You can come up."

With a nod she retrieved the sling and slung it over her shoulders. She stuffed the clip into her pocket.

"Don't pull," she called up to him. "It's easier if I do it myself."

It wasn't as easy as it looked. Or maybe it would have been if she hadn't been exhausted. Her whole body hurt and her shoulder felt as if it were on fire.

It's only twenty feet, she reminded herself as she climbed from one outcropping to another.

"Are you all right?"

She spared a look up and saw Mack staring down at her with a worried expression on his face.

"I'm fine," she lied.

Only fifteen feet to go.

Laura reached for a stunted pine growing out of a small outcropping. The tree leaned into the cliff, forming a deep shadow. As she pulled herself up, she realized the shadow was actually caused by a deep space, a rift between the outcropping and the cliff wall.

The pine tree abruptly gave way under her weight. She grunted with surprise, throwing herself forward to keep from tumbling down the cliff. The tree brushed past her, showering her with clumps of soil and sharp needles. Her shoulder hit the cliff wall, tearing a gasp of pain from her, and she lost her balance, half-sliding into the rift. A sudden horror of getting stuck in the small dark space immediately had her scrabbling for a handhold, anything to help push her out of the rift. Her sleeve caught on something. With an adrenalin-fueled spurt of energy she jerked her upper body out of the rift, freeing her arm.

Something was still caught on her sleeve. She looked down and to her horror saw white bony fingers caught in the folds of her sleeve. With a yelp of fear she yanked her arm away and almost fell off the outcropping when the rest of the skeleton jerked forward in response to her tug.

A skull stared back at her from the other side of death.

"Jesus!" She flailed at the thing with both hands. Shreds of tattered plaid cloth flapped back at her, barely covering the bony chest. She glimpsed a big buckle on a leather belt threaded through the remnants of blue jeans draped around bony hips. Then her fingers caught on something and she looked down, terrified she would find them entangled in hair. But it was only a stone pendant on a leather thong, looped around her fingers. She pulled and it came away, crumbling the fragile neck bones. The skull rolled down the chest with a clatter and she screamed, shoving the entire bony horror away from her. It fell back into the rift, but not before she glimpsed the star-shaped crack on the back of the skull. She pulled herself away, her legs wobbly, her heart pounding with horror.

She looked up, expecting Mack to stick his head over the cliff. After a few seconds she realized he wasn't coming. What the hell had he been doing while she was screaming down here? She glanced back at the rift and it stared back blackly. Had she just imagined the whole terrifying episode? Maybe Mack hadn't heard anything because there hadn't been anything to hear.

Laura took a deep shuddering breath. What was happening to her?

She steeled herself for the final haul up the cliff. When this was all over, she would come back and check the rift. But right now she couldn't get away fast enough. She climbed from handhold to handhold, ignoring her throbbing shoulder and trembling limbs. Only a few more feet. Nothing to it.

In spite of herself, she glanced back at the rift.

Standing on the outcropping was the man she had seen the previous day in the woods. His blue jeans were held up by a belt with a heavy buckle. He wore work boots, a woolen checked shirt and a worn leather jacket. Around his neck was a leather thong with a stone pendant.

He smiled gently at her, almost approvingly. Then she realized she could see the cliff through his insubstantial form.

Laura almost levitated up the rest of the cliff.

CHAPTER ELEVEN

The one vivid image Fay retained of that morning was seeing that man fall over the cliff. But the ride into town would forever remain a blur. She vaguely remembered an endless walk to Mack's house and then the agony of being jostled in his truck as Laura barreled down the dirt road. She recalled freezing, even with a wool blanket around her and the truck heater going full blast, and knowing she was going into shock.

She remembered being afraid of dying.

But now she was in a warm hospital bed with a police officer standing guard outside her private room. Mack was being treated in Emergency, and Laura was making a nuisance of herself with police and hospital officials. Fay smiled as she heard Laura's sharp tone in the hallway.

For the moment all was right with her world. She fell asleep.

* * *

"And I'm telling you there were at least two of them!" said Laura, raising her voice.

The nurse at the ward station gave her a warning look. Laura glared back, and the nurse glanced away.

The antiseptic smell that hospitals wore like cheap perfume was beginning to get to Laura. The ward consisted of one long hallway, with the nursing station in the middle and rooms stretching down either side. The walls were a shade of yellow obviously meant to promote cheerful calm. Green, purple, taupe and orange stripes on the floor led to other wards. Nurses and orderlies carried instruments and pushed carts, gliding silently from room to room, pastel-colored and smiling.

Laura took a deep, calming breath and looked from the uniformed policeman to the plainclothes detective. Both stared back at her, stony-faced. "Mack sent one man, Barney Hicklin, on a wild goose chase down the highway, and two guys chased me and Jason out of the *Trib*. Even if one of those two was Adam, that still leaves two killers out there, and I don't see you doing anything to catch them."

The two officers glanced at each other. Laura didn't need special powers to read their thoughts. At Laura's insistence—and out of a sense of self-preservation, she thought snidely—they had placed an officer at Fay's door, but otherwise they seemed inclined to think Laura had made the whole thing up.

"Have you at least found Jason?" she demanded.

"That would be Mr. Howell, ma'am?" asked the detective, her tone carefully neutral.

Laura hung on to her patience by sheer willpower. "Yes. For the third time, that would be Jason Howell."

The uniformed policeman, whose name tag read Robards, finally took pity on her. "Ma'am, we don't mean to seem unsympathetic, but look at it from our point of view." He uncurled a finger. "First, two paramedics and the two officers we sent to locate the alleged body haven't found anything yet. And the only other person who could corroborate your statements is being examined by a doctor. As soon as Mr. Hawkins can answer some questions, we'll be able to proceed." Laura bristled, but the officer seemed unaware of the patronizing overtones of his words.

Robards uncurled another finger. "Second, Mr. Howell's office advises that he's on holidays for a few days and can't be reached. Doesn't sound to us like his life is in danger. And finally, you tell us someone shot at you in town last night, but there've been no reports of shooting." He shrugged.

For the first time in her life Laura understood why people gnashed their teeth. Frustration mixed with anger in her empty stomach and she wanted to snarl.

"He used a silencer," she enunciated very slowly. "If I'm making all this up, how do you figure my mother got a bullet in her arm? How do you think I got this?" She pointed at her shoulder and its fresh dressing. "How do you suppose Mack got hurt?"

Robards looked uncomfortable and glanced at the detective. She returned his gaze impassively. On his own, the policeman forged on.

"The way it looks to me, ma'am," he said, "is that someone got mad and got hold of a gun. There might have been a struggle, say, between yourself and Mrs. Thorsen. When women fight, it's usually over a man—Mr. Hawkins maybe?" He gave her swollen, discoloring eye a knowing look. "Wouldn't be the first time mother and daughter fought over a man. A couple of bullets might have been fired, say, accidentally, hitting the two of you. Mr. Hawkins might have stumbled on the altercation and in an effort to stop you, he might've been hit in the head with something."

Laura lost any hope of self-control. "And you might have been born with brains, but you weren't!" she snapped.

The nurse at the ward station stood up, a grim look on her face, and the policeman in front of Fay's room turned away to hide his grin.

A couple of heads poked out of nearby rooms as people looked for the source of the disturbance.

Robards scowled and looked as if he wanted to slap handcuffs on her. *Let him try,* thought Laura. She'd had enough of this uniformed jackass. Before she could continue listing the man's defects, the detective stepped between them.

"Stu, why don't you go check on Hawkins? If the doc's through with him, bring him upstairs."

He didn't want to go, Laura could tell, but he had enough wit to recognize an order when he heard one. With a sharp nod at the detective, he turned on his heel and headed for the elevator. Laura stared after him, infuriated by the hint of jauntiness in the man's step.

"You've got to forgive Stu," said the detective mildly, turning back to Laura. "He doesn't know when to quit." She was a tall, heavy woman with gray hair cut in a neat, shoulder-length bob. She carried herself with the grace of strength and the assurance of power.

When Laura didn't reply, she sighed. "Tell me something, Ms. Thorsen. You say these people have been after you for over a week, and yet you never contacted the police. Not even last night, after you say someone shot you. Why not?"

Laura's anger deserted her, leaving behind only silence. She couldn't admit to this woman—Harris was her name, she suddenly remembered—that she had turned to the police as the lesser of two evils. Now that Johnny Tucker's people knew where to find her, she had to take a chance on the police. Surely the man couldn't bribe every police officer in the country.

She was saved from trying to find a palatable answer by a muffled ding announcing the elevator's arrival. She looked up as the doors swooshed open and there, striding down the hallway, was Jason.

"Oh, thank God," she whispered.

At that moment, Jason saw her. A grin split his face and he pulled a rolled newspaper out from under his arm.

"It's here!" he cried, unable to contain his excitement. He waved the newspaper at her. "It's all here!"

"That does it," said the head nurse, slapping a file folder down on the desk and rising to her feet. "All of you," she said tightly, pointing at the detective, Jason and Laura. "Off my floor. Now."

* * *

"All I know, Officer," said Mack, "is that the man was chasing Laura down Tutshi Street, shooting at her. If you don't believe me, go check my truck. He shot the back window out." Mack's head pounded with the fervor of an incipient migraine, and all he wanted was to lie down. He wished the doctor would return and make the man go away.

Officer Robards jotted down the information in his notebook. "Thank you, sir, I will. Now, about this Mr. Rhys…"

* * *

Only a smattering of people shared the cafeteria with them, most of them nurses and orderlies on late coffee break. Laura sat on an uncomfortable plastic chair and read every word of the newspaper article. Detective Harris read over her shoulder. The woman smelled of soap and shampoo, reminding Laura that she hadn't bathed in a while. Both women ignored their coffee growing cold on the table, but Jason wolfed down a breakfast of scrambled eggs, sausages, toast and a banana.

Laura's entire article was all there on the front page of the *Whitehorse Daily Tribune,* without a word changed or omitted, and with her byline.

"Any idea if the wire service picked it up?" she finally asked, not daring to believe her ordeal might be over.

"Nope." Jason shrugged. "But radio and television stations are reporting growing interest in gang activities. Apparently the RCMP and the Crown Attorney's office are working on new information and are looking for a key witness." Despite their redness, his eyes sparkled.

He had spent all night on the Internet, sending the story to editors and news people throughout the country. He had also placed the story on the *Trib*'s web page. The story was now in the public domain— Johnny Tucker would be a fool to have her killed. She hoped his hired killers could read.

Detective Harris finally straightened. She had finished reading the article.

"That question I asked you upstairs?" she said to Laura, who nodded cautiously. "I guess I know the answer now." Harris looked grim. "I'll arrange for security until we're sure you're safe. Excuse me, please. I have to make a few phone calls."

She stepped away from the table, pulled out a cell phone and made arrangements for a search for two armed suspects.

Laura watched her for a few minutes, debating whether or not to tell the detective about the skeleton. Her stomach clenched at the memory of the apparition on the outcropping. It was the same man she had seen in the woods, the man from the photograph.

She would wait to talk to Fay before saying anything to the police. She didn't seriously think her mother had anything to do with the skeleton's presence, despite its proximity to home, but...

She would talk to her mother first.

* * *

Laura stayed at the Howell house while Fay and Mack remained under observation overnight at the hospital. Mr. Howell enjoyed the excitement. Laura had to remain available for questioning by the police and—when they finally arrived the next day—the special investigators from the Crown Attorney's office. Police were a constant presence in the Howell home, although they did try to stay out of the way. Laura appreciated the safety they represented, unnerving as it was.

The man who had shot her was found within hours, and he admitted he and Hicklin were the only ones after Laura. And no, he didn't know where Barney Hicklin was.

Laura was inclined to be skeptical, but Detective Harris believed he was telling the truth.

"How can you be sure?" asked Laura. They were sitting in the Howell living room, drinking Seth's homemade lemonade.

Harris shrugged. "There are methods for questioning."

"Methods?"

"Well, yes, techniques…"

"Good cop, bad cop!" exclaimed Laura.

"Excuse me?" said Harris, clearly nonplussed.

"You know," said Laura accusingly. "Good cop, bad cop. Officer Robards gets me all riled up, and you come across all reasonable. Good cop, bad cop."

The detective looked sheepish. "It's a little more strategic than that." She took one look at Laura's expression and grinned. "Mind you, Robards is very good at it, especially with women. He grates. Comes from growing up with five sisters, I guess. It's amazing what a person will let slip when they're ticked off."

Laura almost sniffed with annoyance. She didn't relish the thought of police techniques being applied to her.

"As for the creep who shot you," said Detective Harris, "the only chance he has is cooperation. Tucker can't help him now—in fact, I think he's afraid Tucker will send someone after him. It's in his best interest to cooperate with us and help put Tucker away. And don't worry about Hicklin. We'll find him." She swirled her lemonade absently. "He has to stop for gas somewhere, and we've alerted every gas station along the Alaska Highway. Every RCMP unit in the territory is out looking for him. It's just a question of time."

The rush of activity helped Laura keep her mind off Adam, whose remains had finally been found, much to her relief. She couldn't stomach the thought of returning to the cliff—she didn't know if she ever would. She couldn't even think about Adam without being swamped by anger and regret, and much to her surprise, grief.

But worse, every time she thought of Adam, she thought of the rift, and its skeleton, and the man she had seen, who wasn't a man anymore.

That first night, undressing in the Howells' spare room, she found the stone pendant. She stared at it for a long time before replacing it in her jean pocket. She didn't remember putting it there in the first place.

* * *

Fay and Mack returned home the next day under police protection, while Laura remained in town. Mack insisted on staying with Fay until Hicklin was caught.

Laura answered every question, took every phone call and spoke to every member of the press who contacted her. By the end of the second day, she was talked out. Hicklin or no Hicklin, she was going home.

* * *

"What about your job?" asked Mack. He stirred honey into his coffee, completely oblivious to the amount of caffeine he was about to ingest, mere hours before bedtime. A small white bandage covered the wound on his forehead, giving him a rakish air.

Laura shrugged and took a sip of her herbal tea. It tasted like lukewarm dishwater. "It's still mine, I guess. The publisher called and apologized, although I'm damned if I know why. I don't think he does, either. But the job is mine if I want it, and he's offered to replace my car."

Mack looked unimpressed. "We'll take a picture of your black eye, then you can ask for a raise, too."

Laura's grin faded when she glanced at her mother's back. Fay stood at the sink, staring at the drawn curtain, oblivious to the conversation. Her bandaged arm was strapped securely to her body with a sling to keep it from moving. Doctors had removed the bullet and determined that she had a hairline fracture in the humerus. She refused to take painkillers, stating she wanted her wits about her. Fay hadn't spoken more than three words since Laura's arrival.

What was going through her mother's mind? Was she worried about Hicklin? Laura wasn't. The man must have heard the radio reports or seen the papers. She was willing to bet he was long gone.

The phone rang. Mack was closest, and he picked it up.

"Hello, Detective Harris," he said after a moment. "Yes, this is Mack. They're both here. Really?" He paused for a few moments. "And you're sure it's him? Yes, I'll tell them. Do you want me to tell Stevens and Basingham? All right. Thanks again."

Mack hung up, turned to the two waiting women and grinned. "A car took a bend too fast about an hour south of here and crashed into a tree. There was a fire, but they identified the car as the one Hicklin was driving."

"What about the driver?" asked Laura, her fingers clenched around her cup.

"Dead. The fellow was barely touched by the fire, but he wasn't wearing a seatbelt and the crash battered him around quite a bit. It sounds like Hicklin, right up to the ponytail and the bomber jacket."

"No identification?" asked Laura.

"Nothing. But if you were a hired killer, would you walk around with ID?"

"I guess not," agreed Laura.

For the first time in days, the little knot of tension in her stomach loosened.

"What about those two police officers?" asked Fay, startling them. "Shouldn't we tell them?"

"Harris said she'd call them herself," said Mack. "On their cell phones."

At that moment a familiar knock came at the door and they all looked down. Officer Stevens let himself in with his borrowed key and walked into the living room. He removed his knit hat when he saw them looking down at him.

"Evening," he said. His cheeks glowed from the brisk night. He was dressed warmly in boots, heavy sweater, jacket and gloves. "I guess you heard?"

"We did," said Fay. She seemed to shake herself out of her funk. "Where's Officer Basingham?"

"She'll be right in, ma'am," he replied. His hands twisted the hat, stretching it out of shape. "Ma'am, if it's all right with you, we'd like to finish out the night here. Just to be on the safe side."

"Nonsense," said Fay firmly. "You and Officer Basingham have done a wonderful job but there's no reason to spend another miserable night out there."

Then Officer Basingham arrived and they shook hands all around, said their goodbyes and left.

With a sigh Fay turned to the others. "I'm going to bed. Why don't you stay again tonight, Mack? It's late, your place is cold… I know a mattress on the floor of the sewing room isn't luxurious, but…"

"Thanks, Fay," said Mack. "I'll take you up on that. Your mattress on the floor is a lot more comfortable than my mattress on the floor." With a grin, he wished them both a good night and disappeared into the sewing room.

"I'm beat too," said Laura after a yawn overtook her. She went up to her mother and, placing an arm around her good side, gave her a gentle hug. "Good night, Fay. Sleep well."

Fay smiled and hugged her back.

As Laura settled gratefully into bed, she realized she still hadn't told Fay or Mack about the skeleton. Or the man. She shied away from the memory. Tomorrow. Tomorrow would be soon enough.

Then they could decide what to do about it.

She dreamed she was a child again, and that her father sat by her bed, rubbing her legs, trying to ease her growing pains. As he rubbed, he told her nonsense stories about the man on the cliff being made out of cheese. She giggled and eventually fell asleep to the sound of his murmuring voice.

She felt as if she had barely closed her eyes when the telephone rang. She was the first to reach the phone in the living room. Still struggling with the dregs of sleep, she picked up the receiver just as the answering machine clicked on. After a confusing moment of trying to listen to two voices, she finally turned the machine off.

In the sudden silence, she said, "Hello?"

"Ms. Thorsen?" came Detective Harris's voice.

"Yes, Detective?"

Didn't that woman ever sleep?

"Ms. Thorsen, I want you to listen carefully, and do exactly as I say," said the detective. "We just received a call from the Watson Lake detachment. A man matching the description of the body we found at the crash site has been reported missing by his wife. He had been driving a white pickup back to Watson Lake from Whitehorse. A gas station attendant near Whitehorse reported seeing a white pickup matching the description, heading back toward town."

Laura stood still in the dark living room, trying to make sense out of nonsense. The fire in the woodstove had died out and the cold was creeping in from the windows. Laura's toes curled against the hardwood floor and she shivered in her oversized T-shirt.

"Ms. Thorsen?"

What time was it, anyway?

"I'm sorry, Detective," she finally said. "Could you repeat that?"

Moonlight streamed through the living room windows, but the nearest clock was in her bedroom.

"Wake up, Laura!" said Harris sharply. The tone of voice, coupled with the detective's use of her first name, finally snapped Laura awake. "Pay attention! I'm telling you Hicklin may not be dead. He may already be in Whitehorse. Get out of the house—go to Mr. Hawkins's place. We're on our way, but it'll be at least half an hour."

"But…" Laura still couldn't grasp what the detective was saying. "Why would Hicklin want to kill me now? The story's out—Tucker would be crazy to want me dead."

"Maybe Hicklin didn't ask Tucker," said Harris patiently. "Maybe he doesn't listen to the radio. It doesn't matter. Don't waste time talking. Get out!"

And with a soft click, Detective Harris hung up.

Laura became aware that Fay and Mack were standing in the living room, waiting. Moonlight caught her trembling hand as she replaced the receiver on its cradle. Finally she turned to the other two. Mack had donned his jeans, and his bare chest gleamed in the pale light. Fay stood silently, clutching her bathrobe close to her neck.

"We have to get out," said Laura. "It might not have been Hicklin in the car."

There was just enough light to see Fay's face settle into lines of despair. Without a word she turned around and disappeared into her room.

It took less than two minutes for them to get dressed in the dark and reassemble in the living room.

"Should we drive?" asked Laura, suddenly uncertain.

"Of course not," said Fay. "If he is out there, he'll hear the engine."

"We'll go out the back door," said Mack, "and take the cliff trail."

Laura studied her mother's face in the moonlight. Fay looked old. A wave of foreboding almost swamped her. "Maybe we should wait here," she suggested, trying to keep the fear from her voice. "Harris said the cops are already on their way."

"Do you have any weapons?" asked Mack, turning to Fay. She shook her head and he looked at Laura.

"We could hide in the crawl space," she said. "He'd never find the trap door."

But Fay was shaking her head. "If I'm going to die," she said grimly, "it won't be like a rat in a trap."

And that was that. With dread settling like a shroud around her heart, Laura followed the others through the living room to the back door.

If this nightmare ever ended, she would buy Fay a dog.

It was cold enough for their breath to fog. As they set out on the cliff trail, Laura glanced up. The moon was close to full and the stars were pinpricks of light in a clear sky. Any other time she would have appreciated the display, but now she was busy battling a growing sense of rebellion. She was tired of running. Tired of being afraid. Just plain tired. Her mother didn't want to die like a rat in a trap. Well, Laura didn't want to die running.

Fay and Mack were ahead of her. She couldn't just sneak back to the house—they would turn back for her. But she didn't want to argue, either. Stuck between the need to stay and fight and the need to make sure her mother and Mack were safe, Laura lost herself for a moment. Anger roared through her like the great river below her, filling her senses with its power.

What she really wanted was to have Johnny Tucker's scrawny neck between her hands. Barring that, she would settle for Barney Hicklin's.

She stopped, breathing hard. Mack glanced back. When he saw how far behind she lagged, he paused, waiting for her.

With a silent curse Laura started forward.

A twig snapped behind her and she stopped. For a split second the whole world stopped, too. Then she looked over her shoulder and light blinded her as a flashlight clicked on.

"Where are you going, Laura?" asked a soft voice.

Laura blinked, unable to move away from the pinioning light. Had he seen Fay and Mack? *Get my mother out of here,* she prayed silently. *Get her out.*

"Is that you, Hicklin?" she finally managed to say. "What took you so long?"

"This place is the ass-end of nowhere. Do you have any idea how many dirt roads lead off the highway in this area?"

Why wasn't he surprised that she had expected him? Laura decided to push harder. Maybe if she stalled long enough, Mack would get Fay out of the way. Maybe the cops would arrive in time. And maybe she would sprout wings and fly away.

"Who was the poor sucker in your car?"

The light moved as he shrugged. "Some guy. I just wanted his truck, would you believe?" His tone was amused, and she could almost see him shake his head in wonder. "I had pulled over, and like a good Samaritan, he pulled over to see if I needed help. Imagine my surprise," he continued, "when this guy steps out, with long, blond hair halfway down his back. All I had to do was cut it, put my jacket on him and voila, instant disappearing act."

Laura wanted to close her eyes against the image he had conjured up of a man stopping in the time-honored Yukon way to help a fellow motorist, only to end up murdered.

"Now it's your turn," he said. "How did you know about him? And what are you doing out here?"

Laura shook her head. He wasn't the brightest light in Tucker's firmament. She wondered if she should be insulted that Tucker had sent someone so dumb after her. "You're too late, Barney. The cops are on their way. They warned me you were coming—that's why I'm out here." She paused for his reaction but couldn't see past the beam of light. "You know, don't you, that the RCMP has arrested your boss? Your buddy's in jail and he's talking for all he's worth. And Adam is dead. It's all over." She took a deep breath. "Turn around and leave, Barney. You still have a chance to get away."

Hicklin was silent for a long time. Finally he lowered the beam a fraction, easing the strain on her eyes. When they finally stopped watering, she saw that he was smiling. She also saw for the first time the gun held in one unwavering hand.

"You're very good, Laura," he said, shaking his head. "You almost had me there. But if Mr. T. had wanted a change of plans, he would have told me." He tapped the back pocket of his pants, where he presumably kept his phone. "No more fooling around. You can jump from that cliff or I can push you. Which will it be?"

The conversational tone of his voice chilled Laura more effectively than the night air. Her remaining bravado dissipated like mist. How had she even considered attacking this man? He killed the way people flossed their teeth—as a matter of routine. What did he have planned after he killed her? A nice meal? A good night's sleep?

"What if I run, Barney?" Her voice was so low she could barely hear herself above the rumble of the river.

"Then I'll shoot you," he said. "Either way, you're going over that cliff. Look at it this way," he added cheerfully. "At least if you jump, you have a chance."

A sudden image of the skeleton in the rift flashed through Laura's mind and she shuddered. Never. She wasn't going to die that way. Just as she was about to make a break for the trees, the light suddenly left her.

"What the hell is that?" Hicklin muttered.

To her amazement, Hicklin had his back to her and was sweeping the trees with the beam of the flashlight. He was looking for something. He turned sideways, crouching, with both arms extended. One hand held the gun, the other held the flashlight just above the gun.

Laura eased herself silently off the trail. The moment she was in the trees, she felt better. Hicklin was still sweeping the flashlight around. A shadow moved at the edge of the light and Hicklin jumped. A man suddenly appeared in the beam's light. With a gasp Laura recognized the man she had seen on the cliff and in the woods.

A shot rang out, and the man disappeared. Hicklin ran to the spot and shone the light about. "Where did he go?" he muttered. Laura remained very still for fear of attracting his attention. When he shone his light away from her, she began moving away again.

"Got you!" cried Hicklin.

Laura stopped in sudden terror. But it wasn't her Hicklin had found. She glanced back. He was now within the trees, too, on the edge of the cliff trail. His flashlight illuminated another figure.

Laura's blood seemed to stop running for the endless seconds it took to recognize her father.

"Daddy," she whispered. The flashlight's beam followed as he moved purposefully toward Hicklin.

Laura's legs gave out and she slid to the ground, scraping her hand against the bark of the tree. She stared at her dead father, unable to grasp what she was seeing. His hair was fuller and he looked younger, but impossible as it was, he was James Thorsen.

Laura was dimly aware of Hicklin staring slack-jawed at the apparition. "Who're you?" he demanded. But even from her vantage point, Laura could see the beam of the flashlight playing through her father's figure.

"Holy shit," came Barney Hicklin's whisper from the trees.

And then another figure appeared at her father's side—the stranger, the one from the cliff. He and her father strode toward Hicklin with the inevitability of fate.

"Stop!" Hicklin shouted. They were less than ten feet from him when he started shooting. When they kept walking toward him, he dropped the flashlight to steady the pistol with both hands. "Son of a bitch!" he screamed as the hammer finally clicked on the empty chamber. He threw the gun. It sailed harmlessly through her father and Barney Hicklin moaned in terror, wrapping his arms over his head and turning away from the apparitions.

Into the sudden silence came the crashing of underbrush and Mack's bellowing charge. Laura looked around in time to see Mack hurtle out of the trees and launch himself at Hicklin.

The air whooshed out of the killer as Mack landed on him, with Fay right behind him.

CHAPTER TWELVE

I almost feel sorry for Hicklin," mused Mack from his favorite seat at the kitchen table. He stirred more honey into his coffee and tasted it. Sweet enough. He put the spoon down and drank.

"Why?" asked Laura, stifling a yawn. She brought her coffee to the table and sat down. For a split second Mack felt as if the last few hours hadn't happened. Except for a tightness around her mouth, Laura looked none the worse for having been up most of the night. Well, that and her black eye. He resisted the urge to rub his gritty eyes.

Detective Harris had finally left with Hicklin, taking with her the last of the police cars. They had arrived moments after Mack had subdued the killer, too late to do more than arrest the man and place him in the back of a cruiser. Thank God Fay lived on twenty acres, or they'd have nosy neighbors to contend with, too.

"You heard him, didn't you?" said Mack, startling Laura. She looked as if she'd forgotten what they were discussing. "Babbling away about the ghosts who jumped him?" Mack shook his head. "I think he's lost it. Or maybe he was always crazy. Maybe you have to be crazy to do what he does for a living."

The sound of the shower downstairs stopped. Fay would be out soon.

Laura sipped her coffee and they sat quietly for a moment, enjoying the peace. "By the way," she finally said, "thanks for saving my life."

He grinned. "Think nothing of it." He waved a hand carelessly. "I've grown fond of the Thorsen women. It wouldn't do to lose one of them." To his surprise he found that it was true. He was fond of mother and daughter, and wanted them both in his life.

The door to the bathroom slid open, letting out a great billow of steam. Mack looked at Laura, remembering the last time he had showered here, the first time he had met her. He wanted nothing more than to hold her, but a sudden shyness held him back. He didn't know what she wanted. Despite their one kiss, she'd been treating him more like a brother than a potential lover.

Fay stepped out of the bathroom and looked up at them. With her hair slicked back and her face freshly scrubbed, she looked much younger. But the smile she gave them did little to conceal her exhaustion. Mack's heart lurched as he watched the woman slowly climb the stairs to the kitchen. He glanced at Laura and found her watching her mother, her eyes suspiciously bright.

It was time to leave these two alone.

He stood up, scraping his chair noisily along the floor. "I should get back to the house. I think the roof trusses are being delivered today. Or was that tomorrow?" He shook his head, amazed that he had lost track of time. He turned to Fay. "Will you be all right?"

"Of course," she said calmly. "One good night's sleep and everything will be fine."

He smiled and gave her a quick, careful hug. She was a hell of a woman. "I'll come check on you later."

"Come for supper instead," countered Fay.

Mack nodded and turned to Laura. "If you have nothing better to do later on, I still have one wall to build before the trusses can go up."

Laura laughed, although it seemed forced. "Sure. I'll be there in a bit. I suppose I'll have to bring lunch, too?"

Mack smiled. "That would be nice." He leaned over and kissed her on the lips.

When he finally released her, Laura was blushing. Her lips looked moist and inviting and he controlled an urge to do it again.

Brother, indeed.

* * *

In the end Fay accompanied Laura to Mack's. Despite the battered state of the work crew, they managed to get the last wall up before the trusses arrived. Fay stood back while the crane deposited each truss precariously on the walls. Laura and Mack, each on a ladder, secured the truss to the walls, and then the entire operation was repeated for the next one.

When the sun began to set, Fay went back home to get supper ready. She took the long way back, down the driveway, up Wild Rose Lane and then onto her long driveway. She walked slowly, enjoying the contrast of warm sun on her back and cool air on her face. Soon she would have to keep a fire going in the woodstove. Her first winter without James.

James. She scrubbed at her eyes, refusing to cry. Last night, in the trees, she had seen him and Sawyer working together to save her daughter. As furious as she was with James, she had loved him, and he had loved her.

To see them together… To know they had both been looking out for Laura…

A sob shuddered through her and Fay stopped in the middle of the road. She wrapped her arms around herself, rocked by grief, and joy, and anger.

* * *

After supper Laura stood next to her mother in the doorway, watching Mack walk down the driveway toward the road. Thanks to the full moon and the porch light, the beginning of the driveway was well lit. Mack turned before the final curve and waved at them. They waved back and watched until he disappeared.

The night was clear and cold. It would dip below freezing again tonight. Maybe there would even be northern lights. By silent consent, mother and daughter stayed on the porch long after Mack was gone, quietly enjoying the night. The visit was drawing to a close. Laura had to be at Johnny Tucker's arraignment in Montreal in two days.

Laura tucked her cold hands inside her jean pockets. Her fingers felt for the stone pendant and traced the metal wire circling it. The leather thong grew pliant again under her fingers.

Even the rumble of the river did little to disrupt the sense of peace that had finally settled over the house. Laura took a deep breath of cool air tinged with wood smoke and released it slowly. The polished gray stone of the pendant felt heavy in her hand. Finally she turned to her mother.

"How long have they been here?"

Fay didn't even pretend to misunderstand. "Since your father died." She sounded relieved to finally be able to say it.

"Who is he?" she asked softly.

Fay sighed and looked up at the sky. Tears glistened in her eyes. "His name was Sawyer Leduc. He was a friend of ours before you were born."

Laura nodded. There was more to this story and it was time she learned it. "The other day," she said, "when Adam died, I found a skeleton in the cliff."

Her mother turned to stare at her, her expression unreadable. Laura told her about the skeleton she had found as she climbed back from shrouding Adam's body.

"There was a pendant," she finished. She pulled it out and handed it to Fay.

Fay stared at the pendant for a long time. Finally Laura realized her mother was crying. She gently pushed Fay down on the top step and sat down next to her. She placed a hand on her mother's.

"Is it your friend I found?"

Fay nodded. She seemed unaware of the tears rolling down her cheeks. "I gave it to him. All those years…"

A woman didn't give a man a gift like that unless he meant something to her. Something more than a friend.

"Mom?" she said gently, not knowing how to ask. "Sawyer was the man in the picture? Did he live in the old cabin?"

Fay remained quiet for so long that Laura thought she wouldn't answer. She stared at the pendant cupped in her hands, crying. Laura put an arm around her mother and held her while she grieved.

"Never mind," said Laura after a while. "You don't have to say anything." Her mother's secrets were her own. She didn't have any right to pry into them.

Fay sat up straighter and wiped her cheeks. "No," she said finally. "It's time you knew."

But she lapsed into silence again, as if marshalling her thoughts, and it was a long time before she spoke again. The cold had worked its way through Laura's sweater and she shivered.

"James and I were building the house—this house. We were going to get married. Then Sawyer came to the Yukon. He'd just finished college and wanted to see the North. He had no family. No ties. He rented the cabin and the three of us became friends. And Sawyer and I fell in love."

Fay looked at Laura. "We didn't plan it, and it's not that I stopped loving your father," she said. "I still loved James. But Sawyer… Sawyer and I…" She shrugged, unable to find the words. "It was a hard, wonderful summer, but so confusing… I spent a lot of time with Sawyer. He had studied geology and he loved tramping through the woods. He taught me about rocks." She clenched a fist around the pendant. "I gave him this one, had it made into a pendant for him." Her eyes closed and she took a deep, steadying breath. "By the end of the summer I was pregnant."

Laura's world shifted beneath her.

"Who…?" She couldn't finish the sentence.

Fay laughed bitterly. "That was the question, wasn't it?" She closed her eyes. "I didn't know who your father was. It took all my courage to finally tell James that Sawyer and I had been lovers… and that you might be Sawyer's child. He was so hurt." Tears squeezed out of her closed eyes. "But I had to tell him."

"What about Sawyer?" asked Laura, unable to contain herself. "Did you tell him?"

Fay nodded. "After I told James, I went to see Sawyer at the cabin." Fay's face changed as memory took over. She seemed younger, as if the years fell away to reveal the girl she had been. "He was thrilled. He didn't care who the father was. He wanted me to go away with him. He said he loved me, and wanted to make a family with me."

The tears fell unheeded down Fay's cheeks, and Laura wiped her mother's face with the sleeve of her sweater, unwilling to interrupt the story to fetch some tissues.

"I loved him with all my heart, but loving him meant betraying James. I was scared... I didn't know what to do. Sawyer was so understanding. He told me to think about it. He would come to the house that night and talk to James, then come for me at my apartment in town. That was the last time I ever saw him."

Laura's mind reeled from the revelations. Sawyer—the mysterious occupant of the cabin—the man who fell over the cliff...

"How did he end up...?" She waved at the river.

"It was a rainy night," continued Fay, oblivious to Laura's turmoil. "I don't know why they were both out on such a night... I guess they had to have it out. But he fell. All those years, I thought he had changed his mind, left me behind—but he didn't. He didn't." She fell silent, pressing the pendant against her heart.

Blood pounded in Laura's ears until she thought she would faint. "How do you know what happened?" she asked. "Did Dad...?"

Fay glanced at her. "I saw what happened, yesterday afternoon. They relived it for me."

Laura digested the information slowly. "So Dad... All that time..."

Fay nodded. "Yes. He knew what had happened to Sawyer and he never told me."

Laura struggled against the feelings suddenly boiling up in her. How could Dad have done that? How could he have left Fay wondering, all those years...

She shied away from thinking too deeply about it. Dad...

"Why didn't you tell me?" she said finally. "About them haunting you, I mean." Laura felt as if her insides were filling with ice water. How could she be sitting on the porch of her mother's house, discussing ghosts?

Fay laughed harshly. "Until you saw Sawyer in the woods the other day, I thought I was going crazy. I certainly wasn't going to advertise the fact."

Laura was having trouble breathing, and the small hairs on the back of her neck were standing at attention. She stood up and went down the stairs, unable to sit still. She paced a few feet down the driveway, and then returned to stand at the foot of the stairs.

"Why didn't Mack see them?" she asked. "And why did Hicklin?"

Fay shrugged. "I don't know. Maybe you have to be attuned to them, or sensitive in some way."

"Hicklin? Sensitive?" It was Laura's turn to look skeptical.

A small laugh escaped Fay. "Good point. I don't know, Laura. Maybe they wanted Hicklin to see them, to distract him. You do know you'd be dead now if not for them?"

Laura nodded. It was hard to accept, but there it was.

Why had Dad and Sawyer been haunting Fay? Why work together in death when they had been rivals in life?

"I didn't tell the police about the skeleton," she finally said.

Fay sighed. "We need to get him out of there. Bury him properly." She wiped her face with her hands. "He was here all along," she murmured. "I guess James's death triggered his appearance."

And then she knew. She knew why Dad had been haunting Fay, why the three of them had remained intricately linked for over thirty years. Guilt. James Thorsen—however indirectly—had been responsible for Sawyer's death. And for over thirty years he had carried the weight of it, unable to tell the woman he loved for fear she would leave him. As for Sawyer, love had held him here. Who knew why it took Dad's death to trigger his appearance. Maybe they gained strength from each other.

Laura glanced up at her mother, but Fay wasn't looking at her. She was staring at the moon, her face a study in grief. Questions would have to wait.

"Mom?" she said gently. "Let's go to bed."

* * *

At two in the morning, Fay gave up on sleep and got up. She moved silently through the kitchen, put some milk on the stove and waited for it to warm. Only the light over the stove was on, its glow warm and welcoming. She pulled out the brandy and put a dollop in her cup before sitting down at the table. Her reflection stared back at her from the window. There was half a night to go before dawn came.

She drank warm milk and thought about the two men in her life. Sawyer had loved her, and she had loved him, but that was a long time ago. James had stayed, loving her, in spite of all she had put him through.

Alone in the middle of her kitchen, Fay Thorsen took a hard look at herself and admitted that she had been cruel.

She had waited until she was sure Sawyer wasn't coming back before agreeing to marry James, and even then she made it clear she was only marrying because she was pregnant. How had he felt, all those years, knowing he was her second choice? She had condemned him for monopolizing Laura's affection, but could she blame him? Hadn't she punished him all those years for not being Sawyer?

Her one comfort was that their last years together had been happy. Once Laura left home, she and James had turned to each other and rediscovered the companionship of their early days. It was a good time.

Then she thought of Sawyer being trapped in the cliff rift for thirty years and grief welled up in her again. James hadn't known. He couldn't have known. He and Laura had climbed all over those cliffs for years. He wouldn't have if he'd known Sawyer's remains were hidden in the rift. He must have searched and, not finding Sawyer, assumed he had been carried away by the river.

And he never told her. Never told the police. James had probably been afraid she would leave him if she knew how Sawyer had died. He had probably feared she would blame him. He had probably been right.

And now? Now she was older, and tired. Her two loves were dead, and it was time to get on with her life.

Raising her cup in a toast to her reflection, she whispered, "I forgive you, James my love, if you forgive me."

She drained the cup and went back to bed.

* * *

The next morning, Laura and Fay worked in the garden, pulling plants and preparing it for spring.

Laura crouched on her haunches, yanking up dead marigolds and brussels sprouts. Her body ached from the hard work she had done on Mack's house. Hopefully the garden work would warm her up and ease the aches.

Fay kneeled at the far end of the garden, in the broccoli bed. Laura smiled to see her mother push a wisp of hair away and leave a streak of dirt on her forehead.

As she worked, Laura went over all she had learned about her mother's past. She wouldn't have thought anything could displace her fear of Johnny Tucker, but she had barely spared him a thought since waking up. She stole another glance at her mother. In spite of the dark circles under her eyes, Fay looked at peace with herself.

"Mom?" she finally asked, her tone diffident. Fay looked up and Laura asked the question she most wanted answered. "Who was my father?"

Fay looked Laura in the eye. "James was your father, Laura."

Laura studied her mother's face carefully, trying to understand what her mother wasn't saying. Then she had it.

"You didn't know for sure, did you?" she said with awe. "All this time, you didn't know. And then you saw the picture." She paused, thinking it through. "It was Great Aunt Gertrude. When you realized I was the spitting image of Dad's great aunt, that's when you knew I was his daughter, not Sawyer's."

Fay was past tears, it seemed. She merely nodded.

Laura was still trying to work it out. "But Dad knew. Or at least he knew ten years ago when he gave Mr. Howell the pictures. That's why you freaked out, isn't it? Why didn't he tell you? Was he punishing you?"

Fay shrugged. She looked frail suddenly, as if she would snap if too much pressure were applied. But that was wrong, Laura knew. Her mother was stronger than Laura had ever suspected.

"If he resented me, it was with good reason," said Fay. She sighed and sat back on her heels. "Your father was hurt, but he was a good man, and he loved me. I don't think he left you the pictures to hurt me. I think he just wanted you to be absolutely sure, in case the question ever came up. I think he didn't tell me because it truly didn't matter to him anymore. You were his from the moment you were born."

A weight she hadn't even been aware of lifted from Laura's shoulders. It was true. Her father had loved her. No matter what other parts of her past might be subject to change, that part wasn't.

"What about you?" she asked finally. "Did it matter to you?"

Fay smiled gently. "I loved you from the moment I knew you existed. Yes, I cared about who your father was, but it never changed how I felt about you."

Laura smiled too, uncharacteristically at a loss for words. She resumed digging and sorting through her new past.

Had Dad unconsciously kept her from Fay as a punishment? Or had he feared that Fay would leave him one day, and wanted to make sure Laura never would? Had he chosen rock climbing as a subtle punishment for Fay? How many ways had he made her pay over the years, perhaps without realizing it?

Laura shook her head slowly. Too much. It was too much to think about right now. And she wasn't even sure she had the right to go down that road. Those questions belonged in her mother's psyche, not hers.

* * *

Mack considered his supply of nails and two-by-fours and wondered if he had enough to finish the day. Maybe he should drive into town now before the lumber supply store closed.

"Hello, the house!"

Mack looked up to find Laura striding down the driveway. "Hey," he called, waving a welcome. He hoped his grin wasn't as foolish as it felt. He watched hungrily as she made her way to the house. He had consciously stayed away from the Thorsen women, knowing this was Laura's last day at home. But now Laura was here, and his heart rate speeded up just at the sight of her.

"Hey yourself," said Laura, walking up the planks to join him. She was dressed in jeans and a heavy sweater. Her hair was up in a ponytail and looked like burnished copper in the sun. He wished she would let it down. The black eye had faded to shades of yellow.

"It's beginning to look like a real house," said Laura, admiring the roof.

He had spent all morning working on cladding the roof and was only a quarter of the way done, but still, he appreciated her encouragement.

"By the time you come back, I'll have rooms." To his surprise, a pang of regret shot through him. He didn't want her to go. He didn't want this prickly, stubborn, beautiful woman to walk out of his life.

Laura turned away from him and studied the view out of the framed window. That would be the kitchen, he noted automatically, moving to stand behind her.

"I'll look forward to it."

"Laura…" He stopped, not knowing what he wanted to say. Then she turned to face him, her eyes bright and he decided words would only get in the way. He placed one hand on her cheek and kissed her. She tasted faintly of coffee and something else, something heady, intoxicating. Then her mouth parted and he groaned, stepping into the kiss and pulling her closer with his free hand. She responded by pressing herself against him and putting her arms around him.

Desire flamed though him and his kisses grew more passionate, his hands running up and down her back, pressing her closer. She gasped and he immediately pulled back, but she pulled him to her again. Her teeth nibbled his lower lip and he ached to cup her breasts in his hands.

If he didn't stop now, he never would.

With something akin to physical pain, he stepped back, pulling out of her embrace. She looked at him, her eyes half-lidded with desire, and he fought down the primitive instinct struggling to answer that look.

He was unable to conjure up a laugh or even a light-hearted comment. "If you're not careful, Laura May Thorsen, I'll take you right here on the floor."

The look she gave him almost made him reach for her again, but he controlled himself. Deep breaths, he reminded himself. He took another step back.

"And that's not what I want," he said firmly.

"You don't?" she said, her voice still smoky with passion.

"No, that's not what I mean." He reached for her arm and pulled her to him, holding her gently. Her hair smelled wonderful, of shampoo and sunshine. He undid her ponytail and spread her hair around her face, running his fingers through it for sheer pleasure. He stopped when she closed her eyes and turned her face up to his.

"I want you more than I've ever wanted anyone," he said thickly, kissing each feature and memorizing it. "But I want all of you. I want to know you, and I want you to know me. I'm your mother's neighbor— we'll be seeing each other for years. We should be very sure we don't regret anything we do. I want the first time we make love to be special, not something we do in the middle of a construction site." He looked around at the unfinished house and managed a grin. "You deserve better than a butt full of splinters."

Laura sighed and opened her eyes. "I'm coming back for a visit at the end of the month. Do you think the house will be finished then?"

Mack laughed out loud and hugged her. "I'll make sure it is," he said, and kissed her.

Laura broke the embrace before passion could ignite them again. "Exactly what makes you think I'd be the one to get a butt full of splinters?"

* * *

The next morning Mack drove Laura to the airport, much to Fay's relief. She didn't think she could handle the farewell without tears, even though Laura would be back for a visit in only a few weeks. There was so much she wanted to tell her daughter, now that the dam had burst.

But all that could wait.

Fay reached for her light jacket and slipped it on. It was time. She closed the door behind her and stood looking out at the day for a few minutes. The temperature was dropping, in spite of the bright sunshine. A faint aroma of wood smoke wafted over her and she sniffed with pleasure. It was a lovely day, a fine day in which to be alive.

Fay chose the cliff trail. She set off down the path, enjoying the brisk wind stinging her cheeks and the sound of the river rumbling far below her feet. She stayed far from the edge to avoid seeing the river. As long as she kept her eyes on the trail, her fear of heights only added spice to the journey.

When she got to the spot where Adam Rhys had fallen, she paused. This was where Sawyer's remains had been. She didn't linger. He wasn't there anymore. The police had removed his remains and there would be an inquest in a few weeks. She would petition the coroner to release him to her for burial. He deserved that, after all this time. She turned away and strode down the path toward the old cabin.

Her first sight of it almost brought tears to her eyes. She hadn't been back to the clearing in over thirty years. She, Sawyer and James had spent so much time here… Now it was a shell, its sod roof long dead, its broken windows staring back at her blindly.

A movement caught her eye and she turned slowly. James and Sawyer stood at the edge of the woods, staring at her.

"It's time for you to go now," murmured Fay. "I'll join you when my time comes."

Sawyer had been the passion of her youth, their love made tragic by his disappearance. But James was the love she had grown into and grown to appreciate. She belonged to both of them, just as surely as they belonged to her.

"Go," she whispered. "Let me be." They turned away, slowly walking toward the trees. They glanced over their shoulders at her, then at each other. Finally they walked into the trees and were gone.

Fay stared at the trees for a long time. Then she turned and headed home.

THE END

About Marcelle Dubé:

Marcelle Dubé grew up near Montreal. After trying out a number of different provinces—not to mention Belgium—she settled in the Yukon, where people still outnumber carnivores, but not by much. Her short fiction has appeared in a number of magazines and anthologies. Learn more about her and her published work at www.marcellemdube.com.

Dear Reader,

Thank you for reading On Her Trail. I hope you enjoyed it. If you did, please consider leaving a review wherever you purchased the story, or on Goodreads.

Reviews are valuable, no matter what rating you give the story. Reviews make the book more visible in online stores and give potential readers a sense of whether or not they would like to read it themselves.

If you would like to join my mailing list to receive (very) occasional updates on my upcoming novels, short stories and writing news, please drop me a line at marcelle.dube@gmail.com.

You can find me on Facebook here: https://www.facebook.com/marcelle.dube.3 and on Twitter here: https://twitter.com/marcelledube?lang=en. And my web site is at www.marcellemdube.com. Come visit.

Thanks, and happy reading!

Marcelle

KEEP READING FOR CHAPTER 1 OF
GHOSTS OF MOROCCO

GHOSTS OF MOROCCO
by Marcelle Dubé

CHAPTER 1

Vancouver, British Columbia—February 2011

Rain in Vancouver usually fell like a benediction on dry skin, a mist depositing sparkling gems on hair, a conduit for the perfume of flowers… in other words, atmosphere.

Except in February.

In February, rain in Vancouver consisted of fat, cold raindrops that fell with a splash to ruin shoes, fog glasses, and dampen even the thickest jacket. Only a wood fire could chase away the dampness that came with a Vancouver rain in February.

"Must you stare out the window like that?" asked Lucie, her secretary and Adler Events' receptionist, without turning around. "The rain has stopped."

Hope started guiltily and crossed her arms against the chill from the window, still clutching the rolled-up copy of Maclean's Magazine.

She smiled at the top of Lucie's impeccably styled gray bob.

"You might as well be my mother, Lucie. You always know what I'm thinking." She had been staring out the window of the tiny waiting room for the last ten minutes. Lucie was right. It had finally stopped raining even though pregnant clouds still loomed over Burrard Street.

Lucie twisted in her chair to look at her, one thin eyebrow arched over her blue eyes. "I am not clairvoyant, très chère. You are predictable." She turned back to her screen. "Now, stop hovering over me and go back to work."

Hope rolled her eyes. She wasn't predictable. She was steady. Dependable.

Stable.

Oh, God. Now she was a boat.

Lucille Marcotte, receptionist and right-hand woman, glanced back at her and smiled in sympathy, laugh lines crinkling at the corners of her eyes. "Chérie, if you do not like the rain, why on earth did you open your business in Vancouver?"

Hope sighed. Every winter she asked herself the same question. Born in Madrid, raised in Dubai, Buenos Aires, Cape Town, and Rabat, she had not known cold, damp winters in her thirty-one years until she settled in Vancouver, Canada. Only Reykjavik had been worse and she'd only been there two weeks.

Three years she had lived in Vancouver as owner of Adler Events, and every winter she missed the warm Moroccan breezes of her youth. She hadn't worn a dress since October. She glanced down at her practical, gray woolen pantsuit and the red silk blouse beneath it, and longed for bare legs and sandals.

For a moment, she couldn't quite remember why she had decided to set up her event management business here.

Finally she said, "The art, the food, the people, the fashion, the mountains, the festivals, the ocean, the work, and oh, yes… It's beautiful in summer."

Lucie's gaze caught on the magazine in Hope's hand and understanding filled her eyes. "I read the article," she said. "Your friend is walking a narrow path through a minefield."

Hope nodded. Salah Abdoulah, King Abdoulah II of Morocco—but just Salah to her—was indeed walking a dangerous path.

"All right," she said. "Back to work." She headed past the little kitchenette to her office at the back and sat down at the maple desk. Lucie was right. There was a lot of work to do.

But her gaze strayed to the windows. As owner of Adler Events, she had cavalierly appropriated the corner office on the main floor of the turn-of-the-century walkup. She could see Burrard Street from one window and a glimpse of Broadway from the other. Both windows displayed the same fat raindrops dripping noisily from the eaves.

February in Vancouver was not for anyone prone to depression.

With Carson and Frédéric gone, it was just her and Lucie in the office. It was too quiet, giving her too much time to brood. Right now, Carson was inspecting the Queen Victoria ballroom for the Cohen wedding reception and Frédéric was on a honeymoon cruise to the Bahamas, where it was definitely warmer than here.

But not as warm as Morocco...

Enough. It was time to work. She had deliberately cleared her morning to finalize the Yukon Quest file. She needed to make a few phone calls to ensure that everything was in place for the Germans for whom she had organized the tour.

She had never understood the attraction of sled dog races, frankly, despite Uncle Hans competing in the Yukon Quest every year. The Germans and the Japanese in particular were fascinated with the Quest—"The Toughest Sled Dog Race in the World"—and the Iditarod.

In fact, it was thanks to Uncle Hans that she'd had the idea of working with a travel agent to arrange tours for the Germans, to start with, and then the Japanese, who were also fascinated by the northern lights.

She had known there would be interest in winter tourism in the Yukon. But, still, she didn't get it. Both races were held in well-below-zero temperatures. Well below.

As she pulled the Yukon Quest file toward her, she caught sight of the trio of Berber chairs she had inherited when Dad died. She loved their triangular lines, brass nails, and leather-covered wood. They always woke a longing in her. Of all the places she had lived as an embassy brat, Morocco was the one that always called to her—in spite of everything that had happened there.

She shook her head. It wasn't surprising that Morocco was on her mind. The Globe and Mail and Maclean's had been musing for weeks on whether or not the Moroccan parliament would adopt the Berber Manifesto and create a separate Berber homeland. The vote was in one week.

It was a stressful time for the country and for King Salah Abdoulah, Rashidah's beloved husband and Hope's friend.

The pain caught hard and tears pricked her eyes. Seven months after Rashi's death, she still felt like someone had punched her in the stomach every time the memory caught her by surprise.

Lucie appeared at the door, donning her three-quarter-length red woolen coat and black leather gloves. Undaunted by Vancouver's weather, she wore high heels and a black skirt and pink sweater set, complete with pearls at her neck. With her tall, thin, elegant body, she looked like an aging model. "I'm off for lunch, then," she said. "Would you like me to bring something back?"

"No, thanks," Hope shook her head. "I brought lunch today." Soup. The perfect food for a miserable winter day. Lucie left with a quick wave and Hope finally opened the file.

Moments later, the outer door opened and Hope smiled to herself.

"What did you forget?" she called, not looking up from the spreadsheet.

When silence greeted her, she looked up, waiting expectantly for Lucie to appear at her door, exasperated that she'd had to return to fetch whatever she had forgotten.

After a moment, Hope called, "Lucie?" Perhaps she'd heard her leaving, rather than returning? She pushed away from the desk, the chair rolling loudly on the laminate floor. A shiver unaccountably traced its way up her scalp.

Such a goose. Dad's words rang in her head, chiding her for her groundless fears. She went to the door of her office and looked out at the reception area. A tall, dark-haired boy stood sideways to her in the lobby, dressed in khaki pants, runners, and a rain-spattered navy rain jacket. It was such an ordinary outfit that her glance slid past his face as she searched behind him for his mother or father.

Then he turned and looked at her and her stomach dropped.

"Meddur?"

Surprise rooted her in place. The last time she had seen the twelve-year-old was seven months ago, at Rashi's funeral. He was at least two inches taller now and looked so much older that it wasn't surprising she hadn't recognized him at first. His thick, dark hair was disheveled and his pale brown eyes bloodshot. Then she noticed the pallor underlying the boy's normally swarthy complexion. They stared at each other and still she couldn't make herself move toward him.

"What are you doing here?" She glanced at the closed door. "Is your father with you?"

Meddur shook his head. His eyes were unnaturally large in a face grown lean so that his jawline seemed sharper. He glanced at the door, as if expecting someone to come in at any moment. Hope waited but he didn't speak.

"Meddur?" she said gently. Something was very wrong with him. How had he gotten here, alone, from Rabat, half a world away?

When in doubt, Dad used to say, feed them.

"Have you just arrived from Rabat?" she asked, forcing herself to move closer. He nodded jerkily. Well, that was progress. "Would you like something to eat?"

He shook his head.

She did a quick mental calculation and came up with ten o'clock at night in Morocco. She would call Rabat. If Salah wasn't there—why would he leave Morocco at the eve of such an important vote? Why would he let his son travel alone?—then she would call Ottawa. Oncle Tabat, Rashi's uncle and Meddur's great-uncle, had recently been appointed as Moroccan ambassador to Canada. She had no idea if he was in Canada right now, but the embassy would know.

Meddur's gaze was fixed on the door. There was something glazed about his look and when she looked closer, she realized he was trembling.

Do something, she told herself sharply. She came closer to the boy, trying to see if he was injured. She didn't know him well, but remembered him as more self-possessed and better-mannered than most adults she knew. He was the son of Rashidah Lamis Abouda Salah and King Abdoulah II, after all. Like Hope, he had grown up in a diplomatic environment. That training didn't shake easily, even at twelve. At least, not normally.

She wished Lucie was still here. She would know what to do—she had grandchildren around Meddur's age.

Just as she reached out to take him by the arm, Meddur finally looked at her again.

"They may have followed me," he said, his voice much deeper than the last time she had heard it.

Hope glanced at the door. "Who?"

"The men," he said, still in a low voice. "The ones who killed Ahmed."

Hope's eyebrows rose and she peered more closely at him as her hand closed on his arm. His jacket was wet with rain.

Ahmed? The Ahmed who was Salah's chief of security? She remembered him as a big man with kind eyes. How could he be dead? Her hands began to tremble. None of this made sense.

"Sit down, Meddur," she said firmly. He wasn't making any sense. "I'll call your father."

"No!" He pulled out of her grasp, surprisingly strong. He was still much shorter than her six feet, but there was an added breadth to his shoulders that hadn't been there at Rashi's funeral. "You must not call him." He was breathing faster now, his brown, thick-lashed eyes blinking rapidly as if to forestall tears.

Hope breathed through the tightening in her chest. Why didn't he want her to call his father? Had he run away from home? All the way to Canada? That was ridiculous. And why would he come here? Because she and his mother had been best friends? He barely knew her.

How could a twelve-year-old boy travel so far alone? Or had he been with Ahmed? Who was now dead…?

His face tight with wariness, he edged toward the door, on the verge of bolting.

"All right." She lifted a hand to show him she wasn't going to grab him. Then her gaze caught on the wash of pink on her hand. What was that?

All at once, it all came together. She looked at the boy and turned her palm out to him.

"Is this blood?" The words came out as a croak.

Meddur nodded and this time, tears did fill his eyes. "Ahmed's blood." The tears spilled over, tracking down his cheeks. "He died protecting me."

Protecting him. Hope shook her head in confusion. "Where? Who killed him? How did you get here?" And why did he need protection?

Meddur didn't seem to notice the tears streaming down his face. "At the airport." He took a deep breath and the tears stopped. "We had to transfer planes. Two men were waiting for us." He scrubbed his cheeks with the heels of his hands. "They had guns. They were going to shoot me. Ahmed told me to run. Then he stepped in front of me and they shot him." He looked at her fiercely. "He's dead."

Hope finally remembered to breathe. She stared at Meddur in horror. All the questions had been swept clear of her mind, leaving behind only one certainty.

"We have to call the police," she said. She turned toward Lucie's phone. "Your father must be going crazy—"

"No, Tante Hope!" Suddenly Meddur was by her side, his too-big hand clutching her right arm. "You can't call anyone—"

Hope picked up the handset. "Meddur, they shot someone." She dialed 911 with her left hand. Suddenly, Meddur released her and made a dash for the door.

"Meddur!"

"Nine One One Operator," said a voice over the telephone. "What is your emergency?"

Meddur flung open the door and ran out. Hope hesitated a split second as the operator repeated the question, then she dropped the handset and ran out after Meddur. He was already halfway down the block, running toward Broadway. If he got there, she would lose him in the lunchtime crowd.

"Meddur, wait!" She ran down the stairs, clinging to the banister to keep from sliding on the slick steps in her smooth soles. "Meddur!"

A white Civic drove by, followed by a green van. The man in the passenger seat of the van turned to look at her as it passed by. Hope reached the sidewalk and ran after Meddur, splashing through puddles and trying to avoid the leaves made slick by decomposition and rain.

Her longer legs had the advantage over his youth and swiftness, but she was hampered by the slippery leaves.

"Meddur!" He didn't even look back at her. He was almost at Broadway. A couple walking on the other side of the road stopped to take in the chase. Then the green van screeched to a stop just ahead of Meddur, its wheels throwing up water on the cars parked along the sidewalk.

Meddur glanced over his shoulder at the noise and put on a burst of speed, but it was too late. The side panel door of the van opened and a man leaped out just as the passenger door opened to disgorge the man who had stared at Hope.

She stumbled to a stop, her hands clamped over her mouth in horror as fifteen-year-old memories stabbed through her.

Then one of the men caught Meddur by the arm and began dragging him toward the van. Meddur yelled, struggling in the man's hold, and then another man reached him and grabbed his flailing arm.

Meddur fought harder, and finally Hope snapped out of her paralysis.

"Leave him alone!" she cried, running as fast as she could toward the men. The one from the passenger seat spared her a dark-eyed glance but kept pulling the boy toward the van. Just then a car screeched to a stop behind the van and the driver jumped out.

The two abductors had reached the van and were trying to force Meddur inside but he braced his feet against each side of the opening and resisted.

She finally reached the man from the passenger side, grabbed his arm, and tugged on it with all her strength, pulling him off balance.

"Whore!" The familiar accent caught her by surprise and she faltered. The man freed his arm and pushed her away so hard that she lost her footing.

She landed hard against an Audi and almost slid to the oily pavement before catching her balance.

Then the stranger from the car pounced on the man still holding Meddur. At the same time, the driver of the van climbed out to help his partners. Everything became a blur of shouts and flying fists.

Suddenly, Meddur freed himself from his captor. Hope darted in, snatched his hand, and pulled him out of the melee.

"Come on!" she cried, pulling his hand as she began running back to the office.

Meddur darted a glance over his shoulder at the fighting men and tightened his hold on her. They were almost at the stairs to her office when she realized one of the men from the van was chasing her—the driver.

"Faster!" She put on speed and pounded up the stairs, Meddur right behind her. They ran into the office and Hope slammed the door shut behind her. She let go of Meddur's hand long enough to shove the bolt shut. At that moment, the man slammed into the door, making it shudder. He tried the handle and then looked at her through the window. For a second, they stared at each other through the gilt lettering. She had an impression of dark skin, black hair, and pale brown eyes. The hate in his eyes held her to the spot. Still holding her gaze, he reached into his pocket.

Meddur pulled on her hand. "He has a gun!"

Hope whipped around, grabbed Meddur's arm, and ran into her private office. She grabbed her purse and coat from the coat stand just inside the door and a second later ran back out.

In the entryway, the heavy glass window shattered noisily, startling her. She glanced back to see the man using the butt of a very big handgun to clear the shards out of the frame. Then he reached in to unbolt the door.

Hope didn't wait to see any more. With Meddur on her heels, she ran toward the back of the office, past the washroom and the kitchen and to the back door, which led to the alley where she and Lucie parked their cars. She fumbled with the lock and finally got the door open.

It opened onto a metal landing and a short flight of stairs that led to the alley. The door clanged when she slammed it shut. The smell of garbage hung in the humid air.

"Go!" She pushed Meddur toward the stairs. "The blue Honda." She pointed at her car, then had a horrible split second when she thought she had left the keys on the credenza behind her desk, but they were in her coat pocket and she gave them to Meddur. "Unlock the doors and get in!"

Without waiting to see if he obeyed, she dragged the raccoon-proof metal trash bin toward the door and placed it where it would tip over when someone opened the door. It might delay pursuit for a few precious seconds.

Then she ran down the stairs. Behind her, the door flew open to crash against the railing. As she reached the rough pavement of the alley and ran for the car, the trash can clattered down the metal stairs with a sound like crashing cymbals, followed by a string of colorful curses in Tamazight.

Tamazight. The language of Morocco's Berbers.

Meddur had unlocked the car doors and was sitting in the front passenger seat, twisted to see what was going on behind him. He reached across the driver's seat and opened the door for her just as she reached for the handle. Hope slid into the seat and reached for the ignition before she even closed the door. Meddur grabbed her coat and purse and pulled them out of her way.

The keys were already in the ignition. "Good," she muttered as she turned the key and started the car. Then she slammed the transmission into drive and stepped on the gas, her tires leaving rubber on the dry pavement beneath her car.

"He's going to shoot!" cried Meddur. "Get down!"

Hope glanced in the rearview mirror and saw the man standing in the middle of the alley, legs braced, both hands on his pistol. The pistol jerked up just as her driver's side mirror exploded into shards of glass and plastic.

Then she shot out of the alley onto Broadway and was gone.

END OF EXCERPT

NOVELS BY MARCELLE DUBÉ

Mendenhall Mystery Series:
The Shoeless Kid
The Tuxedoed Man
The Weeping Woman
The Untethered Woman
The Forsaken Man

Backli's Ford
Ghosts of Morocco
Jilimar
Kirwan's Son
Obeah
On Her Trail
Shelter

www.ingramcontent.com/pod-product-compliance
Lightning Source LLC
Chambersburg PA
CBHW020847260626
47169CB00003B/1181